ENDLESS LOVE

A SWEETGUM MEADOWS STAND-ALONE ROMANCE
BOOK 8

IMANI PRICE

First Edition: January 2025

ISBN 978-1-960207-62-3 (ebook)
ISBN 978-1-960207-63-0 (paperback)

Published by Books to Hook Publishing, LLC.
www.BooksToHook.com

CONTENTS

Chapter 1   1
Chapter 2   7
Chapter 3   16
Chapter 4   20
Chapter 5   26
Chapter 6   31
Chapter 7   39
Chapter 8   44
Chapter 9   55
Chapter 10   62
Chapter 11   73
Chapter 12   83
Chapter 13   90
Chapter 14   97
Chapter 15   116
Chapter 16   123
Chapter 17   130
Chapter 18   146
Chapter 19   156
Chapter 20   161
Chapter 21   165
Chapter 22   171
Chapter 23   179
Epilogue   185

Author's Note   191
Also by Imani Price   193

CHAPTER ONE

*A*lex Zhang couldn't remember the last time he'd been truly happy. He'd almost grown used to the dull ache in his chest, like background noise that wouldn't quit. Even working at his parents' Chinese restaurant—a place he used to love—felt more like wading through quicksand than anything else. On the surface, the cheerful hum of customers and the scent of sizzling stir-fry made it seem like business as usual, but inside, Alex felt hollow.

Still, he tried not to let it show.

He stood behind the counter, hands folded in front of him, meeting a wave of requests as politely as he could manage.

"Can I get another pair of chopsticks with mine?"

"My sweet and sour sauce ran out. Could I grab another?"

"How much is an extra bowl of rice with today's special?"

"Would it be okay if you took a picture with me and my friends?"

He responded to each one in turn, forcing a gentle smile despite the fatigue weighing down his shoulders. "Of course— here you go," he said, handing out chopsticks and sauce. "Extra rice is two dollars," he added for the next person. Then his gaze fell on the teenage girl peering at him over her phone.

A self-conscious heat crept into his cheeks, but he mustered a friendly tone. "I'd love to, but we're almost ready to close, and I'm running around like crazy," he explained, an apologetic smile tugging at his lips. "Next time, though, okay? Enjoy your meal!"

The girl looked slightly disappointed but nodded, giggling with her friends as they walked off. Alex exhaled, turning to the older gentleman behind her. "I'm so sorry, sir. Did you say you wanted water with your meal?" He mentally counted the handful of customers left in line. Only two more after this man. Relief flickered through him as he noticed his father stepping to the door to switch the sign from 'open' to 'closed.'

Almost there, Alex thought, rolling his shoulders as he took the man's order. Closing time felt like a finish line he couldn't wait to cross. And if his superficial grin and steady voice fooled everyone, that was fine by him.

His next customer stepped up, and Alex blinked in recognition. "Jamal?" he asked, forcing the corners of his mouth upward. They had been friends in high school, though Alex had to admit he wasn't really in the mood for a stroll down memory lane. Too many old faces in a town this small.

"Hey, Alex! Thought that was you." Jamal's grin was genuine, and Alex felt a twinge of guilt that he couldn't quite match his friend's enthusiasm.

"Yeah, I've been helping out my parents from time to time," he said, leaning forward on the counter to hide his restless energy. "Hard to avoid old classmates when you're back in Sweetgum, huh?"

Jamal laughed. "No kidding! But I hadn't run into you until now. Guess the rumors that you were back are true."

Alex felt the gaze of the remaining customer behind Jamal and decided to cut the reunion short. "Let's get your order in before the kitchen closes. We've got a nice curried chicken special today."

Thankfully, Jamal picked up on his gentle brush-off and placed his order without pressing for details about Alex's return. The last thing Alex wanted to talk about was his divorce—especially not here, in front of everyone. He still wasn't sure how to explain something that still made his chest tighten whenever he thought about it.

Once the final customer was served, Alex cleared the counter, spraying disinfectant on the smooth surface and wiping it in broad, practiced strokes. The steady rhythm calmed him, letting him focus on something other than the swirl of thoughts in his head.

"Ah, my wonderful son," his mother teased as she stepped out of the kitchen. Mrs. Zhang's warm smile radiated pride, her eyes creasing in the corners. Pots clanged behind her, and the faint melody of the mop swishing across the floor gave the place its usual cozy bustle.

Alex half-laughed, half-sighed when she patted him on the back. "You're just happy I didn't stay holed up in the house all day."

"And that you helped us handle this busy rush. We might have to ask you to come by more often." She winked. "You draw in the younger crowd, and who knows—maybe one of them will be your future wife."

His mom's playful matchmaking made Alex's stomach flip. "Mom," he groaned, tilting his head in mock exasperation as he set the rag aside. "We've been over this. I'm not... it's just not the right time."

She didn't look convinced, her expression settling into the familiar, hopeful look that said she would love nothing more than to see him find love again. Before she could press further, a shuffle of hurried steps announced his father's arrival.

"*Kung Pow, Enter the Fist* tonight!" Mr. Zhang said, as if the very thought of it made him feel twenty years younger. He mimed a silly series of kicks in the empty restaurant aisle. "Let's have a family movie night!"

His mother beamed. "Yes, Alex, join us! Unless you'd rather head home to watch something all by yourself, looking glum," she teased, raising a brow.

Though Alex's first instinct was to decline, he recognized an olive branch when he saw one. In the grand scheme of things, an evening with his parents—who only wanted to cheer him up—wasn't so bad. "Alright, alright," he relented, a small, genuine smile lifting his lips. "I'll meet you both at the house once I finish up. Sounds like fun."

"That's my boy!" His dad clapped him on the shoulder, then reached for his apron. "Lisa, we're out for the night—lock up when you're done," he called to the cleaner.

Alex couldn't help admiring how easily his parents turned the page on each day. If something didn't go their way, they tried something else. If they were sad, they found a new reason to smile. Meanwhile, he was stuck in neutral, replaying every painful detail of his failed marriage.

But for all his brooding, he still loved these two more than anything.

When his parents disappeared into the back office, likely to gather their things, Alex let out a slow breath. *If only I could be as optimistic as they are,* he thought. But until he figured out how to let go of the hurt still lodged in his heart, he'd just keep swimming along in the family stream, doing what he could to make them happy.

He gave the now-gleaming counter one final swipe, turned off the lights behind him, and let himself sink into the solace that came with closing time. He was far from healed, but at least here, in Sweetgum, he didn't have to pretend life was perfect.

And for tonight, that might be enough.

LATER THAT NIGHT, Alex paused mid-stroke on his digital tablet, design stylus hovering just above the screen. He realized he'd been staring at the same half-finished layout for a while now, without making any progress. With a soft sigh, he set the tablet aside and leaned against his headboard, letting his thoughts drift back to the evening.

They'd eaten noodles and sipped soda while re-watching the same silly kung fu parody his dad had dubbed their "family movie." The memory drew a faint smile to Alex's lips. Nights like that were becoming rare—lighthearted moments that made him feel almost…normal. But he also knew such warm scenes came packaged with inevitable questions. The older he got, the more his parents took up matchmaking as their new favorite hobby, hinting that it was time to find "the right one."

He closed his eyes and rubbed at the tension in his forehead. Peripherally, he noticed Odie curled up on the floor beside the bed. Even half-asleep, the dog looked utterly content, tail twitching in some dream chase. Alex reflected on how he'd filled Odie's food bowl to brimming before going to the restaurant tonight, worried the dog might get hungry. Of course, Odie still devoured the extra leftovers Alex had brought home. Spoiled as he was, Alex couldn't be happier to indulge him. A good dog deserved good meals.

Odie stretched and shifted, and Alex gave a little chuckle. "Tired, huh, buddy?" he murmured, his voice echoing in the stillness. Even the simplest moments—like watching his dog sleep—grounded him in a way he desperately needed these days.

The divorce had been… well, brutal. In the end, Alex had managed to keep his partial ownership of the family business and, most importantly, Odie. Almost everything else was gone—tangible reminders of a life that had unraveled too quickly. He dreaded the thought of explaining it to each new face he encountered in Sweetgum, so he chose not to. Small-town folk had a way of piecing stories together, and his mother's penchant for chatter ensured most people already knew the basic outline anyway.

With a weary sigh, Alex turned off his tablet and let it rest across his lap. Today had at least been more eventful than yesterday, when he'd slept in far too late and barely left the couch. Lately, his routines blurred into each other: morning workout, freelance projects, quick lunch, then sometimes heading over to help at the restaurant. Day in, day out—like clockwork.

Yet as tedious as it felt, a part of him wondered if a bit more excitement might be exactly what he needed. A small spark, something to jostle him out of his rut. The heaviness in his chest wouldn't vanish overnight, but maybe—just maybe—he could find a hint of hope somewhere in the daily grind.

He gave a short, rueful laugh and reached to flick off his bedside lamp. Tomorrow morning, he'd be up early to design a few more layouts and, if luck was on his side, bury himself in enough work to keep his regrets at bay.

For now, he pulled the blankets over his lap, listening to Odie's soft breathing. In this quiet, peaceful space, it was just him and his dog—and, for the moment, that was enough.

CHAPTER TWO

$\mathcal{M}$aia fiddled with the plain gold ring dangling from the delicate chain around her neck, her fingers tracing every curve of the metal like a soothing ritual. She stood in what used to be her Aunt Dianne's kitchen, the soft light of the overhead fixture casting a warm glow on faded wallpaper and a scuffed floor. The house felt eerily quiet, a far cry from the days when her aunt's laughter would fill these same walls.

She could already sense Aimee's footsteps echoing down the hallway—those signature heels tapping on the wooden floor. *Always running a bit late,* Maia thought, an affectionate smile ghosting over her lips. *And yet somehow, always arriving in style.*

Aimee appeared in the doorway, trailing her fingertips along the wall. "It's nice," she said, tilting her chin to study the lighting. "Really nice for a place that's been… neglected so long."

The word "neglected" stung like a sudden slap of cold air. Maia's stomach twisted, and she prayed her flinch went unnoticed. "I agree," she answered, forcing an even tone. "All it needs is a thorough sweep and some dusting. Then it'll look more like home." With a brisk nod, she moved away from the kitchen counter to stand beside Aimee. "I'll probably come by tomorrow morning before my jog to tackle it."

Aimee pivoted on her heels. "You sure? You're doing everything on your own so early? I know you're a morning person, but even morning people have limits."

As they moved toward the front door, Maia's gaze lingered on the path to the living room—where she could almost see a younger version of herself racing down the hallway, Aunt Dianne greeting her with a plate of freshly baked cookies. The memory played like an old film reel, winding through her thoughts until Aimee's sudden clap jolted her back to the present.

"Right," Maia murmured, trying to recover from the emotional whiplash. "I'm not planning to do it all in one day. Just the kitchen first… then I'll see how I feel."

She forced herself to look at the fraying carpet on the stairs, lined with dusty family photographs. Each picture reminded her of the warmth Aunt Dianne once brought to every gathering, and how empty it all felt now. *That's why it took me so long to come here,* she admitted silently. *I wasn't ready to face a house so full of memories and so devoid of her.*

Aimee's shoulder bumped gently against hers in a silent show of support. They halted by the front door. "Starting small is good," Aimee said, her tone a careful blend of encouragement and concern.

For a moment, silence hung between them like an unspoken question. Then Aimee squeezed Maia's shoulder. "Hey," she said softly.

A dampness blurred Maia's vision. She blinked hard, willing her tears away. "I'm fine," she insisted, inhaling deeply. "Tomorrow I'll wake up early, listen to my affirmations, and get back into a positive headspace."

Aimee didn't look entirely convinced. "Crying is okay, too," she reminded Maia, her voice kind. "But since you're all about bright sides, remember Aunt Dianne left this place specifically to you. She trusted you to keep her memory alive, and now you're finally here."

The encouraging words made Maia's chest tighten. She let her friend's hand slip from hers, nodding in agreement. "I know," she whispered. "It's just… it feels like I'm losing everyone. First Derek, and then—" She paused, swallowing the lump in her throat. "But you're right. I need to focus on the fact that this house is a gift. Aunt Dianne wanted me to have a safe place to remember her."

Bracing herself, Maia flicked off the kitchen light and locked the door behind them, stepping onto the porch. A gentle breeze tugged at her braids, and she shivered—not from cold, but from the swirl of memories still clinging to the house's walls.

Aimee followed her to the edge of the unkempt lawn, where a single streetlight illuminated the sidewalk. "You're not losing everyone," she said, nudging Maia's arm lightly. "You still have me."

Maia shot her a lopsided grin. "And I'm grateful. Really." She led the way to her compact car, rummaging through her purse for the keys. Street after street in this neighborhood was quiet at night, something that felt both comforting and a little eerie. *Olive Lane—the hub of early bedtimes and retiree gossip,* she mused.

As they reached the vehicle, Maia started to voice the tangles of her thoughts. "It's just that, with Derek and—"

Aimee cut her off, waving a dismissive hand. "Nope. Not going there." She pointed a playful but stern finger. "I refuse to let you spiral on my watch. Are we clear?"

Warmth flickered inside Maia. Aimee's presence was strong, a cushion against the old heartbreak that still sometimes threatened to swallow her whole. "Okay, okay. Let's just head out," she conceded, sliding into the driver's seat. Aimee hopped in on the passenger side.

They buckled in, and as Maia pulled onto the main road,

Aimee began her usual pep talk. Each word was a lifeline. Maia nodded, letting her friend's encouragement wash over her. She reminded herself that she'd come a long way already—she just had to keep moving.

"I'll journal about this tonight," Maia said after a stretch of quiet. "Get all my feelings down on paper."

Aimee nodded vigorously. "Yes. You say it yourself: no bottling up emotions. Manage them. Confront them head-on."

A hint of a smile curved Maia's lips. *She sounds just like me.* Over time, her friend had adopted some of Maia's motivational mantras. Hearing them echoed back in Aimee's voice felt comforting, a reminder that there was someone out there who truly understood.

A glint of gold caught Maia's eye in the rearview mirror— the ring swinging gently at her throat. Aimee always insisted she should ditch the necklace, especially after everything with Derek. Maia couldn't. She didn't wear it out of longing but as a sobering reminder that love wasn't always a fairy tale.

It hurts, but it keeps me real. She'd learned the hard way that blind optimism could lead her straight into heartbreak. Aunt Dianne's death—and the inheritance of this big, empty house— was just another blunt reminder that life didn't pause for anyone's grief.

Finally, Maia reached Aimee's subdivision, the headlights sweeping over tidy lawns and flower beds. Aimee squeezed Maia's arm one last time before unclicking her seat belt. "You good?"

"Yeah," Maia answered, nodding firmly. "I'm fine. Thanks for… all of this."

"That's what friends are for," Aimee sang out, leaning in for a quick hug. "Text me if you need anything, okay?"

"Will do." Maia watched Aimee unlock her front door, stepping inside. Only when the porch light blinked out did Maia drive on.

Her thoughts wandered as she navigated quiet streets. *Now to head home,* she mused, the word forming a slight ache in her chest. Home was a tricky concept. She had her own place now—this inherited house—but stepping inside still felt like intruding on memories that weren't entirely hers.

Maybe tomorrow morning's jog will help. Jogging was her salvation, her mental reset button. She'd head over to Aunt Dianne's place first, do a little cleaning, then hit the pavement. One foot in front of the other, heart pumping, lungs full of fresh air—her best way to cope.

"Routine," she murmured, gripping the wheel. "I just need to stick to my routine."

A small, determined smile curved her lips as she merged onto a quieter road. Because at the end of the day, that routine —those early runs and her daily mantras—had carried her through heartbreak and loss. They could carry her again. And maybe, if she found the courage, this house could become something resembling a true home—rather than just a painful reminder of what she'd lost.

For now, that was enough.

EARLY THE NEXT MORNING, Maia tugged the trunk closed with a dull thump, breathing in the crisp pre-dawn air. Two rolled rugs lay nestled inside, ready for laundering—just the first of many tasks in her ongoing effort to restore her late aunt's house.

She brushed off her palms, then turned toward the imposing two-story structure she'd come to dread. Even bathed in the faint glow of a streetlamp, it was impossible to ignore its peeling paint and shuttered windows. A lump formed in her throat, mingling with guilt and nostalgia she couldn't entirely shake. *I should feel grateful,* she reminded herself. *This place is mine to cherish now.* But loss clung to every corner, making the house feel both comforting and lonely at the same time.

A sudden gust of wind blew her braids across her cheeks, snapping her out of the reverie. With a firm tug, she gathered the strands into a high bun. Glancing at her phone, she noted the time—just after five a.m. *No time to stand around,* she told herself. *Stick to the routine.*

And so she did. She set off at a brisk jog, letting the rhythm of her sneakers on pavement soothe her jumbled mind. The sky was still more gray than blue, the sun barely hinting at its arrival. As usual, running was her lifeline. *Breathe in, breathe out,* she reminded herself, focusing on the cool air against her face and the subtle scent of wet grass.

Still, memories of the cluttered living room she'd swept earlier clung stubbornly to her thoughts. She couldn't quite shut out the image of that faded floral rug—an echo of Aunt Dianne's laughter seemed woven into its fibers. Her heart clenched, but she pushed herself to run faster, as though speed could somehow outrun grief.

Look around, she ordered herself. *Be here.* The residential street was serenely quiet, dew twinkling atop lawns, and a handful of early birds fluttering among the trees. Even the slight bounce of her necklace—a gold band nestled near her heart— felt grounding, if bittersweet. It was a fresh reminder: *Life goes on,* just like the slow rise of the sun overhead.

A few blocks away, the sky had begun to lighten from charcoal gray to soft indigo. Birdsong warbled in the distance, and the occasional porch light flickered here or there. This was precisely why Maia loved these early runs: the quiet calm, the gentle push of cool air against her lungs, and the promise of a day yet to be written.

She turned a corner and immediately slowed, her gaze catching on a lone figure across the street. A jogger—tall and lean, with a purposeful stride that made him look like he'd been running his whole life. His dark hair caught a stray beam of a streetlamp, highlighting strong cheekbones and a firm jaw. Maia's breath stuttered in her throat.

Who is that? she wondered. *He is fine!*

In Sweetgum, she knew enough folks to at least recognize them in passing, yet this man's face was entirely new. He was on the opposite sidewalk, heading in the opposite direction. Though the space between them was a good twenty feet, Maia's heart thumped as if he were right next to her.

He wore a simple hoodie, unzipped just enough to show a T-shirt beneath, his pace measured and controlled. Everything about him—his focused expression, the subtle flex of his arms—radiated confidence. Maia felt a sudden surge of warmth spread across her cheeks, and she had to remind herself to keep jogging instead of gawking.

She heard the faint thud of his shoes against the pavement, matching a tempo that both unsettled and intrigued her. For a split second, she considered raising a hand in greeting. *Why not?* It was a small town, after all. But a ripple of unease accompanied the burst of attraction. She hadn't felt this kind of instant pull toward anyone in a very long time, and it left her more rattled than she cared to admit.

Pretend you didn't notice, she decided, uncertain how else to handle the flutter in her chest. Her ring necklace bounced against her collarbone, a weighty reminder of heartbreak—and a warning that letting anyone in meant risking pain again. Maia drew in a quick breath and faced forward, picking up her pace. She told herself it was because she wanted to push her cardio, but deep down, she knew she was running from the strange, magnetic pull of that stranger's presence.

Out of the corner of her eye, she could see him pass, his attention fixed on the path ahead. *Good,* she told herself, *he didn't notice me, either.* Yet a pang of disappointment nipped at her, no matter how many times she insisted she wasn't interested.

She darted her eyes straight ahead, legs pumping faster. *Focus on the run,* she commanded, letting the drumming of her sneakers soothe the jumbled hum of her thoughts. It seemed to work for a few minutes—until she looked up to find no sign of the man at all. He'd vanished beyond the next block, leaving her with a disconcerting emptiness that was at once a relief and a letdown.

"Breathe," she whispered, forcing a tiny smile of self-reproach. *Getting all flustered over a random jogger? Grow up, Maia.* She was here to ease her mind, not spin herself into daydreams about men she didn't know.

She pushed onward, the early morning air cooling the heat in her cheeks. Another few blocks later, she spotted an overgrown lot across the street—a patch of stubborn weeds and dandelions where Aunt Dianne once told her she wanted to plant wildflowers. Maia paused, resting her hands on her hips to catch her breath.

"Too fast," she muttered with a breathy laugh, glancing down at her shoes. She'd been running harder than usual, adrenaline from that brief encounter still coursing through her. If she was honest, a spark of curiosity lingered: *Would I see him again tomorrow? And why do I suddenly want to?*

Before she could dwell on it too long, movement at the far edge of the block caught her attention. Someone in dark clothing strolled down the opposite sidewalk, hands shoved into their pockets. Unlike the handsome runner, this person's posture bristled with tension—shoulders hunched, head ticking side to side as though scanning for something. A tendril of unease curled through Maia's gut.

Even in a quiet town like Sweetgum, not everyone was as warm as the usual morning dog-walkers. She glanced around, searching for a possible explanation—maybe the person was lost or simply an early riser? But there was something about them that set her on edge. Their gaze flicked in her direction, then away again.

She bit the inside of her cheek, reminding herself that not every unfamiliar face spelled trouble. *It's none of my business,* she concluded, pushing off the weedy patch to resume her run. Still, a part of her itched to keep one eye on this stranger, if only to be safe.

Pulling in a stabilizing breath, Maia forced her feet to move. *If they're not bothering me, I won't bother them.* She veered onto a side street that led back toward her car and, ultimately, her aunt's house. Already, the thought of stepping back into that silent living room made her chest tighten—but she had a full day ahead, and she'd promised herself to stay on schedule.

When she finally risked a glance back, the figure in dark clothes had vanished from sight. An echo of tension lingered in her muscles, but she tried to shake it off. *Maybe they're just an oddball out for a morning walk,* she told herself, though she couldn't help letting out a quiet sigh of relief.

Her mind skittered back to the memory of that jogger—*the* jogger—whose mere appearance had sparked an inexplicable flush. Even if she chalked up her reaction to being caught off guard, she couldn't deny how alive she'd felt in that single moment. Her pulse had beat faster, not from exertion, but from sheer attraction.

It was enough to remind her that she wasn't entirely numb, that something in her still responded to the possibility of connection—no matter how brief or unexpected. The reminder hovered like a soft whisper, trailing her all the way home.

She couldn't decide if it was a warning or a promise.

CHAPTER THREE

"Are you kidding me?" Alex's voice trembled with outrage as he fanned through the thick stack of papers on his home desk. He looked at Phoebe with a mixture of confusion and hurt that bled into anger. "I thought we said we'd work this out. We went to therapy—together. I even gave up my freelance hours to make every session, and now you spring divorce papers on me?"

With a frustrated shove, he rolled back from the desk. "I'm not signing anything," he muttered, teeth clenched.

Phoebe leaned forward, palms pressed against the polished surface. "You're not signing because you know exactly how this'll turn out," she shot back, tossing the papers at him. "We both know this marriage isn't working. It's time to stop pretending."

Alex's laugh came out harsh, forced, as he shook his head. "How can you give up after everything we've invested—time, money, everything—to fix this?" He slammed his fist against the table in frustration. "No. I won't sign."

Her arms folded tight across her chest. "Are you really so attached you can't admit we're over? A grown man should know when to walk away."

"And maybe a grown woman should keep her promises instead of *blindsiding me," Alex shot back, standing up abruptly and circling the desk. Each word came faster, louder, an overlapping echo of anger and heartbreak. Odie's barking erupted from the next room, and somewhere in the back of Alex's mind, he realized things had gotten too loud, too volatile. A red haze clouded his vision, sirens flared outside with blue lights flashing, and suddenly there were uniformed officers at his door. In a chaotic blur, Phoebe stepped aside, phone pressed to her ear as she spoke in hushed tones about Alex's 'out-of-control behavior.' Anxiety crushed his chest. This was all wrong; none of his efforts had mattered... and everything he cared about felt like it was slipping away.*

Alex jolted awake, heart hammering against his ribcage. An empty, dim room greeted him, the early-morning shadows flickering across the walls. He blinked rapidly, trying to dispel the storm of emotions lingering from the dream.

A soft jingle and a curious tilt of the head drew his attention to Odie, sitting beside the bed with ears perked. The dog let out a gentle whimper and pressed his cold nose against Alex's arm in a quiet plea for reassurance.

"Odie," Alex rasped, placing a hand on his loyal companion's back. Odie's tail gave a slow wag, his gaze reflecting nothing but concern. The knot in Alex's chest loosened, if only slightly.

Exhaling a shaky breath, Alex turned his gaze to the curtains. Only a faint glow of morning light seeped through, but any chance of falling back asleep now felt impossible. The divorce. Therapy. The police. It was all behind him—or so he kept telling himself. Yet each nightmare proved that he was still tangled in the past.

Odie nudged him again, and Alex mustered a thin smile. "Alright, boy," he murmured, swinging his legs over the side of the bed. Usually, he was up early to feed Odie and start his day. Today, though, the dream clung to him like a weighted blanket, slowing every motion.

He sat there for a moment, letting the tension ebb. "Let's go," he finally whispered. He was determined to shake off the night's ghosts. Whether it was a brisk walk in the cool dawn air or losing himself in a few freelance projects, Alex would find something—anything—to keep the memories at bay.

Willing himself out of the house felt strange at such an early hour, but Alex decided his mom was right—fresh air might do him good. He let the steady beat of his music fill his ears as he jogged under the muted, bluish-gray sky. Sweat trickled along his neck in the Georgia heat, despite the gentle breeze, but he didn't mind. Each footstep felt like shedding another layer of restless energy.

He passed a few unfamiliar houses, breath hitching as he pushed harder. It amazed him how different the neighborhood looked when most people were still asleep. The hush of morning wrapped around him, offering a kind of peace he hadn't experienced in ages. There were no customers, no coworkers, no forced smiles—just the dull thump of his shoes against the pavement.

By the time he reached a STOP sign near the end of the block, he slowed to catch his breath, hands braced on his hips. His heart pounded, but the cloud of his nightmare was finally lifting. A twinge of satisfaction went through him—maybe he'd found a new coping mechanism. Early morning jogs weren't exactly in his wheelhouse, yet here he was, feeling… calmer.

Until he noticed someone else.

Across the street, another runner emerged from the shadows. She wore a dark blue hoodie and black leggings, her braids woven with golden-brown highlights that seemed to catch the faint morning light. Headphones on, she seemed entirely focused on her own pace—so much so that Alex doubted she even realized he was there.

He paused, curiosity stirring. He wasn't used to encountering other people at this hour, particularly not someone who offered him zero acknowledgment. Typically, in Sweetgum, strangers at least exchanged a nod or small greeting. But this woman breezed by without as much as a sideways glance, and somehow that intrigued him more than if she'd smiled and waved.

Alex wiped his brow, a subtle chill running down his spine that had nothing to do with the cool air. He couldn't help thinking she was beautiful, and the thought caught him off guard. He hadn't noticed anyone like that in a long time—not since before his divorce.

And now, with one quick glance, his nightmare was momentarily forgotten.

He exhaled a laugh under his breath. Maybe getting out of the house had multiple benefits, after all. Shaking out his shoulders, Alex turned to head back home, the emptiness inside him not feeling quite so heavy. He still wasn't sure if he'd discovered something that might pull him out of his funk, but the morning had given him a slice of genuine stillness.

He decided right then that he'd try this again tomorrow. Not necessarily to find her—but he couldn't pretend he wasn't curious if she'd be here again. He wanted to chase after that sense of ease he'd found, however brief it had been.

With renewed energy, Alex set off at an easy jog, smiling softly to himself. For the first time in a while, he felt a flicker of hope—like maybe his path forward was just beginning.

CHAPTER FOUR

Maia toyed with the simple gold ring dangling from the chain around her neck, her thumb brushing over its cool, worn metal. Despite the comforting hum of the busy diner around her, she couldn't shake a tiny flutter of anxiety in her chest. Across the table, Aimee let out a dramatic sigh.

"I wish you would get rid of that necklace," she said, gently pressing her turkey sandwich onto the plate in front of her.

"Why?" Maia's voice was soft, but she knew where this conversation was heading. It was the same talk they'd had countless times before.

Aimee's expression was equal parts exasperation and concern. "Because it's weird, Maia. You're literally wearing his ring like a yoke around your neck."

A reflexive tremor shot through Maia's fingers, and she dropped the ring, letting it rest on her collarbone. "That's not it at all."

"So what is it?" Aimee leaned forward, arching a perfectly manicured brow. "You need new jewelry? Girl, we can go shopping right after this shift—"

"No." Maia shook her head firmly. "I just… need it, okay?"

Aimee held her gaze a moment, searching for some flicker of explanation. When none came, she sighed and resumed picking at her sandwich. "Fine. I still say you deserve something better." Then, her face brightened like a lightbulb switching on. "Let's stop focusing on the bad stuff. You told me there's been a certain someone sharing your running route these last three days?"

Maia found herself rolling her eyes. She set down her fork, the smell of freshly baked pies wafting over from the diner's kitchen. "He's not 'sharing' my route. We just happen to run at the same time every morning."

"Uh-huh." Aimee's honey-hued eyes glittered. "Because that's some big coincidence, right?" She shot Maia a playful smirk. "You've got him interested. I saw this movie once: two early morning joggers keep bumping into each other—bam! True love."

Amused despite herself, Maia let out a small laugh. "You've watched every romantic movie under the sun; of course you'd find at least one with that plot." She paused to take a sip of her water. The ambient chatter in the diner swelled as the lunch crowd filtered in. "Real life is different, though. I wouldn't expect anything… major."

Aimee's unimpressed arched brow told Maia that her friend wasn't buying that. "So what do you think is going on, then?"

Why is she so hooked on this? Maia wondered, studying Aimee's determined expression. "He's probably new in town and decided that five or six in the morning is a good time to run. End of story."

Aimee plopped the remainder of her sandwich onto her plate. "But you *did* say he was cute."

Heat crept up Maia's cheeks like a slow tide. "Yes," she admitted, fumbling with the napkin in her lap. "But that doesn't mean he's deliberately picking my route. And even if he was, it's not like we're destined to be together," she added pointedly, hoping it would douse the spark of excitement in Aimee's eyes.

Unfortunately for Maia, Aimee was relentless. "Hmm," Aimee began, tapping her pink-polished nails on the tabletop. "Then what's your explanation for him sticking around the same areas you do?"

"It's not like I watch his every move," Maia grumbled. She cast her gaze around the room, noticing how many customers had squeezed into the cozy diner. Red vinyl booth seats, squeaking as people shifted, took her back to the first time she and Aimee had come here. She'd instantly fallen for the place's homey charm, just as she had for their chicken pot pie—still the best in Sweetgum, in her opinion.

In truth, she *had* paid attention to the attractive runner these last few mornings. She'd studied the set of his shoulders, the way his dark hair fell across his forehead, and the way his hoodie clung to a lean but muscular frame. She'd never seen anyone quite like him outside of a movie or magazine, and part of her was half-convinced he couldn't be real.

Aimee's voice yanked her back to reality. "Maia?"

"Hmm?" She blinked, catching sight of Aimee's smug, knowing smile.

"It's okay to be into him," Aimee said. "There's no law against being attracted to someone."

Maia sighed, her gaze dropping to her half-eaten pot pie. Derek's ring—the one hanging on her necklace—felt heavier than ever in that moment. "Maybe," she admitted quietly, "but I'm not sure I'm ready. He could be married for all I know."

"Married?" Aimee rolled her eyes, leaning in like she was about to spill a secret. "Why jump to that? Did you see a ring on his finger or something?"

"I... was running pretty fast, remember? Not exactly taking inventory of his hand," Maia joked, offering a shaky laugh. A quick mental rewind of her last encounter with the jogger made her pulse hitch. She could have sworn his fingers were bare—no ring, no tan line, nothing. "I have no idea, Aimee," she finally said, exhaling. "Plus, come on, the guy's like an eleven out of ten. You don't just walk up to that kind of perfection and introduce yourself."

Aimee let out a snort. "Yes, you do. That's exactly what you do if you want answers." Her expression softened. "It doesn't have to be a big romantic gesture. Just start with 'hi' and see if he's open to chatting."

Easier said than done. Maia's heart squeezed with old fears, old hurts. After Derek, she'd vowed never to let her guard down so easily. "I'm not sure I have it in me," she whispered, her fingertips brushing the ring at her throat again. She shut her eyes, recalling how painfully everything had ended. Trust wasn't a simple matter.

Sensing Maia's shift in mood, Aimee placed a gentle hand on her arm. "Okay, maybe I'm pushing too hard," she conceded. "But I'm serious when I say a little conversation never hurt anyone. Making a new friend is a whole lot less scary than starting a relationship, right?"

Maia nodded, the tension in her shoulders easing. *She's right,* she told herself. *Friendship is safe ground.* She rattled the ice cubes in her glass, thinking how she wouldn't mind hearing that runner's voice—knowing his name, what he was doing in Sweetgum. If nothing else, it might satisfy her curiosity. "I guess I could try to say hello. No promises," she added quickly.

"Deal," Aimee said, beaming so brightly Maia couldn't help but smile back.

The clink of silverware on plates drew Maia's attention to a well-dressed older gentleman stepping into the diner. His hair, slicked back with a touch of silver at the temples, caught the overhead light. He smoothed his coat lapels before gliding toward a small table in the center of the room.

Aimee leaned over, lowering her voice. "Ben Walters. He's

sort of a local big shot, right? I thought he owned that bed-and-breakfast by the lake."

"He does," Maia confirmed. She watched as a waitress approached him, though she didn't take his order. It was like she was waiting for something—or someone. "Odd to see him here by himself."

Aimee wiggled her brows conspiratorially. "Rumor has it he only wants Rochelle to serve him. People say he's sweet on her." Her grin turned mischievous as she drained the last of her soda.

Maia's eyes lit up. "That's adorable." She glanced around for Rochelle, the diner's owner, feeling an immediate kinship with this older gentleman who was braving the lunch rush just to see someone special. *If that rumor's true, I hope Rochelle gives him a chance,* Maia thought with a little flutter of her heart. Love stories—especially unexpected ones—always filled her with a cautious kind of hope.

Catching the time on her phone, Maia slid to the edge of the booth. "I should get going. My inbox is exploding, and Aunt Dianne's place still needs loads of work."

Aimee nodded and stood, grabbing her purse. They both tossed a tip on the table. As they navigated through the bustling diner to the door, warm greetings passed between Aimee and the other staff, who teased her for leaving them in the midst of the lunch crowd.

Once outside, a cool breeze ruffled Maia's bun, and she pulled the strap of her handbag higher on her shoulder. They strolled together toward Maia's car, parked a block over on Sweetgum's main street. The sidewalks teemed with locals on their lunch breaks—chatter and laughter weaving through the crisp air.

"I'll see you for dinner?" Aimee asked, drawing out the last word in a hopeful lilt.

"Definitely," Maia said. She paused with one hand on her car door. "And hey—thanks. For… encouraging me." She fiddled with the ring necklace once more, but this time it felt a bit less like a weight and more like a reminder that her past didn't have to define her future.

Aimee's smile radiated warmth. "You got this," she affirmed, stepping back to let Maia climb in. "Even if you just say hi, that's a start."

Maia nodded, shutting the door and rolling down the window enough to return Aimee's wave. As she pulled away, her thoughts drifted to the early mornings and the striking runner who kept showing up on her route. *Maybe just a friendly greeting next time,* she told herself, *no big deal.* Yet her pulse fluttered at the mere idea.

She drove off down the quiet street, sunlight glinting against the windshield. In her chest, uncertainty warred with a flicker of excitement she hadn't felt in a long time. Perhaps it was time for a change—time to face the possibility that not everyone would hurt her like Derek had. Even the ring around her neck seemed to rest a little lighter against her heart.

And for the first time in quite a while, that prospect made Maia smile.

CHAPTER FIVE

It was barely past five a.m. when Alex tightened the laces on his running shoes for yet another morning jog. He took a steadying breath, letting his gaze drift around the living room he'd only recently begun leaving behind at such an early hour. In the corner, Odie whined softly.

"You just ate," Alex reminded the dog, arching an eyebrow. "Don't give me that look." Indeed, the lab mix had just polished off a brimming bowl of kibble and now stood, tail wagging with anticipation, as though he might join Alex for the run.

Guilt prickled at the back of Alex's neck. He crouched to ruffle the fur between Odie's ears. "I know, buddy," he said quietly. "These runs are for my head as much as my body, and… you know you're more of a 'stroll around the block at sunset' kind of dog, right?"

Odie cocked his head, as if not entirely convinced.

Alex pressed a gentle kiss to Odie's snout, then stood. "Tell you what," he promised, easing toward the door, "I'll take you for a nice long walk tonight. We'll sniff out every mailbox in this neighborhood, okay?"

At that, Odie's tail whipped back and forth, and a soft huff of contentment escaped him. Alex's chest tightened with affection—some days, this dog felt like his only real anchor.

"Be good while I'm gone," he murmured, stepping through the squeaky front door. He rolled the sleeves of his hoodie and locked up, the keys jingling in his hand like a tiny bell urging him onward.

Outside, the early morning air cradled him in a cool hush. He relished that fleeting sweetness before July's heat would press down hard. Dawn in Sweetgum was unlike anywhere else: the quiet rustle of leaves, the distant hum of a neighbor's radio, and birds daring to chirp before the sun was fully up. Alex inhaled, letting that freshness settle inside his lungs.

He started his jog on the familiar sidewalk, sneakers tapping a rhythmic beat against the concrete. Just a week ago, the mere thought of facing a new day had felt like a chore. Yet these morning runs were beginning to change that—little by little, they helped him shake off the fog.

He picked up speed as he passed the house where an old-timer was already watering flowers on the porch. The man offered a wave, and Alex returned a nod, a small smile ghosting across his lips. It felt good to move, good to exchange even a brief friendly gesture, and good to notice that he was doing better than he had been.

I'm actually thinking about the future again, he marveled as he pushed onward. Only days ago, imagining anything beyond the week's end had made his stomach twist. But now, questions bubbled up—would he keep freelancing, maybe help with the family business more seriously? He wasn't sure, but it was a relief to even consider the possibility of tomorrow.

Rounding a corner, Alex abruptly spotted someone familiar ahead. His pulse tripped. She was there again, the same woman with brown-highlighted braids who'd breezed past him on several of his runs. Today, her braids were pulled into a ponytail that bounced with each stride, and a deep-blue sweater clung to her arms, matching her sneakers.

He slowed for half a second, debating whether to hang back or pass by. Before he could decide, she glanced over her shoulder. Their eyes met—dark, steady brown meeting his own. Despite himself, Alex's heart lurched.

Embarrassed at the sudden spark of recognition, he sped up. For some reason, running faster felt like a safe solution. He managed a polite nod as he overtook her, hoping his quick wave would suffice. But her footsteps thundered to match his pace, and within moments, she was beside him.

Surprised, Alex halted, trying to catch his breath. She stopped too, turning around with an apologetic smile.

"Sorry, did I startle you?" she asked, running a hand over her ponytail. She sounded winded but cheerful, a shine in her eyes that made him stand a little straighter.

Alex unzipped his hoodie halfway, letting the cool dawn air seep against his sweat-damp T-shirt. "No," he said, swallowing against a sudden dryness in his throat.

A moment of silence enveloped them, only punctuated by the distant caw of crows and the faint scuffle of someone dragging a trash can to the curb.

She drew a small breath. "I've noticed you running lately," she said. "I'm Maia, by the way. I... I guess we have the same route?"

He nodded, forcing himself to meet her gaze. "Alex. And, yeah. I recently picked up morning runs. Helps clear my head." The admission felt oddly personal, but he didn't regret it.

Maia's features lit with understanding. "Same for me, honestly. I'm at a desk all day, so running is my way of keeping myself sane." She paused, hesitating for just a second. "Actually, since we see each other out here so often, I was wondering if you'd want to run together—just to keep each other motivated. Totally casual," she added, voice pitched hopefully.

The offer caught him off guard. His heart pounded uncomfortably, not from exertion, but from a flicker of alarm. A part of him wanted to say yes. She seemed friendly, and there was a warmth to her presence that he couldn't deny. But the protective shell around his heart cracked at the mere idea of letting someone new in.

He found himself shaking his head. "I appreciate it… but running alone works best for me."

The instant the words left his mouth, he hated how cold he sounded. Maia's face faltered for an instant, but her polite smile flickered back in place. "Sure. No worries. Bye, then."

And just like that, she was gone, jogging away with swift, graceful strides that faded into the gray hush of morning.

Alex stood there, rooted in guilt, forcing a breath through clenched teeth. "It's for the best," he mumbled, more to convince himself than anything. He still watched Maia's retreating form until she turned a corner. *She's just a stranger being nice,* he thought. *I'm not ready to be that guy again.*

He was about to turn around and head home—maybe brood over how he'd messed up that interaction—when a jolt of movement caught his eye. A shadow detached itself from the corner of a house ahead, trailing after Maia. The figure's body curved forward like it was trying not to be seen, clothes dark against the early light.

A cold prickle of alarm raced down Alex's spine. His heart, already thudding, kicked into overdrive. He didn't know who that was, but something about the way they moved, creeping in Maia's direction, set off every internal alarm.

"Hey!" Alex shouted, launching himself forward. Everything else—his guarded heart, his plan to stay distant, even the sting of awkwardness—vanished in an instant. He had no clue what the stranger intended, but Maia deserved to be safe. And if Alex could help, he wouldn't think twice.

He sprinted after them, ignoring the ache in his chest. The morning might have started with a promise to Odie and the promise of peace—but right now, Alex only cared about one thing: making sure Maia wouldn't face this danger alone.

CHAPTER SIX

So, he preferred running alone. Maia's cheeks still burned as she replayed Alex's blunt words in her mind. *Was that just a polite way of saying he wants nothing to do with me?* She glanced around the empty sidewalk, her stomach twisting uncomfortably.

She slowed her pace, the crisp morning air catching in her lungs. She couldn't ignore the sting of his rejection. *Had I been too forward by asking him to be my running partner? Too pushy?* Her thoughts buzzed with uncertainty. In Sweetgum, it wasn't unusual to chat with strangers, so why did Alex's reaction feel like such a personal snub?

He must be a loner, Maia told herself, trying to keep her mind from spiraling. Yet something about Alex fascinated her in spite of his curt refusal. *What made him so determined to be alone?*

Trying to focus on the path ahead, she turned her attention back to her usual route. Normally, she'd take a left at the intersection up ahead. Maybe heading home early would help her forget how she'd basically been brushed off. She took one more step, intent on ignoring the flutter of disappointment in her stomach, when a new sound interrupted her thoughts.

Pit-pat, pit-pat, pit-pat—fast, heavy footfalls pounded behind her.

A hopeful flicker shot through her chest. *Could it be Alex? Maybe he changed his mind—* She turned with a tentative smile, only for her heart to seize when she saw someone else entirely.

Dressed head-to-toe in black sweats, the large figure from a few days ago was hurtling toward her. Fear crackled along Maia's nerves. She opened her mouth to speak, but the man was already upon her, his hand darting into the front pocket of her hoodie. His touch felt cold, invasive.

Maia's scream tore through the still morning air. Before she could register what was happening, the stranger yanked something out of her pocket and bolted past her. The violent jolt sent her stumbling, and she landed painfully on her hands and knees. "H-Hey!" she shouted in disbelief, arms shaking. "My phone!" *He took my phone...*

The realization flared in her mind at the same moment her knees hit the pavement. Her breath came in quick, panicked gasps. A swirl of terror and anger churned in her belly. How could this be happening in broad daylight in her safe, quiet town?

Before she could scramble upright, another figure barreled past. Tall, lean, dark hair plastered to his forehead from exertion. *Alex.* Maia's pulse fluttered in shock. *He came back.* She watched, half-stunned, as he sprinted after the thief with fierce determination.

She wrestled herself upright, ignoring the sting on her palms. Everything felt unreal, as though she were watching from a distance. Down the sidewalk, Alex engaged the thief in a brief, chaotic scuffle. Maia held her breath, heart hammering. *Please be okay, please be okay...*

Alex managed to knock the man to the ground, and for a fleeting moment, relief surged through her veins. But the thief wriggled free with unexpected strength, rolling into the street and darting away between parked cars. By the time Alex tried to pursue him, the stranger had vanished.

Maia pressed a trembling hand to her chest. *He got away.* Her shoulders sagged, the rush of adrenaline leaving her dizzy. Had any of that really just happened?

Seconds later, Alex jogged back toward her, chest heaving, a familiar object in hand. *My phone.* Maia exhaled a shaky laugh of relief.

"Are you okay?" he asked urgently, holding out her phone. Concern etched his features, and perspiration glistened at his temples.

Maia swallowed, trying to steady her breathing. "I—I think so." Her knees still throbbed from the fall, and her voice trembled, but she reached for Alex's outstretched hand. The warm press of his palm sent an unexpected jolt of awareness through her. Once he helped her to her feet, she clutched her phone to her chest like a lost treasure. "Oh my gosh, Alex. Thank you. I can't believe you got it back."

She powered the screen on, checking for cracks. "It's… it's still fine." She let out a slightly hysterical laugh, eyes shiny with tears she refused to shed. "You were like some kind of super-hero," she breathed, gazing up at him. His hair, damp with sweat, stuck to his forehead, and something about the fierce focus in his eyes made her heart flutter.

Alex dragged the cuff of his sleeve over his brow, letting out a ragged breath. "I couldn't just let him get away." His voice was low, still threaded with adrenaline. A tentative, half-smile tugged at his lips.

Maia's fear melded with gratitude, leaving a tightness in her throat. She inched closer, scanning the area as if expecting the thief to jump out at any moment. "I don't know how to thank you. That was… you were—" Her voice cracked with relief, and embarrassment heated her cheeks.

He offered a soft shrug, but his gaze flickered protectively over her shoulder. "I just did what anyone else would've done… or should've. I'm glad you're not hurt."

"Me too," Maia whispered, though her knees still wobbled beneath her. The memory of that man's hand in her pocket flashed through her mind, and she shivered, instinctively moving closer to Alex. *She felt strangely safe in his presence, despite the awkwardness of their earlier exchange.*

His voice remained gentle. "Since this place isn't as safe as we both thought, I'm guessing we can't leave you alone out here, can we?" He paused, raking a hand through his damp hair. "I might not be the biggest fan of company on my runs, but I don't want anything bad happening to you, either. Let me come with you from now on—just until this guy is caught."

Something quivered in Maia's chest, part relief, part confusion. *Did he feel obligated to protect her, or… was there something more?* She managed a shaky smile. "Thank you. I—I'd like that. I mean, I'm still a bit freaked out."

Alex nodded, scanning the street as if to make sure it was clear. "Why don't we head to the station? It's only a few blocks away. Reporting this is the best shot at catching him. We can walk, if that's okay."

She swallowed, pushing away the trembling in her limbs. "Yes, definitely," she agreed, glancing at her phone again. Her reflection stared back from the black screen, eyes wide with residual shock. *Is this really happening in Sweetgum?*

As they set off down the sidewalk together, Maia glanced sideways at Alex's profile. He kept scanning the area, clearly on alert. It was the first time she'd gotten a proper look at his features up close—high cheekbones, a strong jaw, and unique dark eyes that hinted at an Asian heritage. His hair, still damp from exertion, clung to his forehead, and she noticed how those sharp angles gave him a quietly intense aura she couldn't ignore.

Her heart gave a small jolt. She'd always thought he was handsome, even from a distance, but now… there was something undeniably magnetic about his presence. The adrenaline no doubt heightened her awareness, but she couldn't deny the surge of attraction buzzing beneath her fear.

"I'm sorry if I'm a little… out of it," Maia said quietly as they rounded a corner. The early sunlight revealed more of Sweetgum's modest downtown area, where shops were just beginning to open. "I can't believe I was almost robbed in broad daylight," she added in a low voice.

"I can't believe it, either," Alex admitted, his tone still clipped with leftover tension. "But I'm glad you got away without injury."

Maia's lip quirked with a frail smile. "I owe that to you." *Her hero,* an unbidden voice inside her mind whispered. The warmth of gratitude rippled in her stomach, and she pushed it down, uncertain what to make of this new version of Alex—cautious, solitary Alex, who had just risked himself to help her.

They soon reached the police station, a modest brick building nestled between a post office and a small pharmacy. Inside, a weary-eyed officer took down their statements. Maia fumbled through her account, details blurred by shock, but Alex filled in the gaps she'd missed. He described the thief's posture, height, and voice with surprising clarity.

When they finally emerged onto the sidewalk again, the clock on Maia's phone read six-thirty a.m. She thought of her day job and the frantic scramble she'd have to manage to make up for lost time. She drew a trembling breath, trying not to imagine the thief lurking behind every corner.

A large man in gray sweats jogged past them, and Maia nearly squeaked in alarm. Alex laid a reassuring hand near her elbow, his gaze full of quiet concern. "You're still on edge," he said gently.

"Yes," Maia admitted, cheeks flaming. "I keep thinking—what if you hadn't been there?"

His eyes softened, an unspoken something flickering across

his features. "But I was," he murmured. Then he cleared his throat, as though embarrassed by the intimacy of the moment. "Look, how about a coffee or something? Sometimes taking five minutes to calm your nerves can do wonders."

She blinked, the tension in her chest loosening a bit. "You really think coffee's going to fix this?"

"Maybe not fix," he conceded with a faint smile. "But at least help." He nodded toward a nearby bakery, its windows glowing with early-morning light. A chalkboard sign out front promised hot pastries and fresh cappuccinos. "They make killer croissants. And scones, according to my mom."

A flutter of amusement rose in Maia's chest. "You come here often?" she teased, surprised at how the conversation made her heart skip a beat.

"Sometimes," Alex said, tucking his hands into his hoodie pockets. "I'm partial to the croissants, but if you want scones, I won't judge."

Maia let out a shaky laugh, her pulse still thrumming from the morning's chaos. "Alright," she whispered, stepping toward the bakery's inviting door. "If you say they're that good, I believe you."

Together, they slipped inside. The scent of warm bread and roasted coffee swept over Maia, easing her tension a notch. She cast a glance at Alex from beneath her lashes. *He'd been so cold earlier. Why go to all this trouble now?* Yet here he was, guiding her to an empty table near the window, his gaze never straying far from her face—like he wanted to be sure she was truly okay.

As they sat, Maia exhaled a cautious breath. Her hands still trembled slightly, but the flurry of adrenaline was beginning to subside. Part of her wanted to pepper Alex with questions— about his life, his reasons for running alone, or how he'd managed that quick takedown. Another part was too over- whelmed to form coherent words.

There'll be time for that, she told herself, stealing a glance at the man across from her. *We're definitely not strangers anymore.*

Despite the harrowing morning, a faint warmth kindled in Maia's chest. Even if she didn't fully understand Alex's motives, the protective concern in his eyes spoke volumes. For the first time, she allowed herself to consider that perhaps his aloofness wasn't about her at all. Maybe there was a story behind his solitary habits… and maybe, just maybe, she'd get to find out.

A LIGHT BREEZE ruffled Maia's hair as she and Alex stepped out of the bakery. The early sun had risen higher, bathing the street in a warm glow that felt strangely peaceful after such a tumultuous morning. She inhaled deeply, trying to let the aroma of fresh bread and coffee linger as a reminder of safety.

Beside her, Alex took a measured breath. "Hey," he said, glancing at her as if gauging her nerves. "Look, I know you might still be shaken up. If you need to head home right away, I get it, but…" He hesitated, something like concern flickering in his eyes. "I'd really like to check on you later, make sure you're doing okay."

Her pulse fluttered in that odd, new way she was starting to associate with him. "Oh?" she managed, stuffing her hands in her hoodie pocket to keep them steady.

He nodded, the corners of his mouth twitching into a tentative half-smile. "My parents own the Chinese restaurant on Main Street—Sweet and Spicy Chinese Palace. They open for lunch pretty early. How about we meet there around eleven? The real rush doesn't start until noon. I can treat you." His tone grew playful. "For, uh… safety's sake."

She couldn't help but smile, warmth displacing some of the leftover tension in her chest. "You sure you're okay with that? I don't want to be a bother."

"Definitely," he replied, slipping his hands into his hoodie pockets. "I'll feel better knowing you're alright. Besides..." He paused, eyes flickering with something like humor. "You might like the food."

Maia laughed softly. "In that case, I'm in."

Alex nodded. "Sweet and Spicy Chinese Palace. You can't miss it—bright red sign." He shifted his weight, casting her a final, almost shy glance. "See you later?"

"Yeah," Maia answered, releasing a breath she hadn't realized she'd been holding. "See you."

They parted ways at the sidewalk, Maia heading east while Alex turned west. She hugged her arms around herself, smiling faintly. *What a morning.*

She still wasn't entirely sure what to make of Alex, the aloof runner who'd come to her rescue in more ways than one. But something told her that meeting him again, this time on purpose, was a step toward a future that might be brighter than any she'd dared to imagine lately.

CHAPTER SEVEN

This wasn't exactly how Alex had predicted his morning would go. He'd started the day looking forward to a quiet run, lost in his own thoughts, and now he was ushering Maia—practically a stranger, yet somehow not—into his parents' restaurant. The midday sun cast a warm glow through the windows, and a comforting aroma of frying chicken and fresh vegetables wrapped around them the moment they stepped inside.

Still, in spite of the unexpected turn, a small part of him *liked* how things had unfolded. As jarring as the robbery had been, it'd given him a reason to spend more time with Maia—and to find out she wasn't just another face on his jogging route.

"Come on," he said, guiding her toward the worn front counter. "It's early enough that we'll get served right away." He glanced over his shoulder, noticing how Maia clung to the strap of her bag as she looked around, taking everything in. It gave him a twinge of satisfaction to share this piece of his life with her—especially after the chaos she'd been through that morning.

His father, Mr. Zhang, appeared from the back of the restaurant, wiping his hands on a towel draped over his shoulder. "Alex? What are you doing here?" He paused to squint at Maia. "And who's this?"

"Dad, meet Maia. She's... had a rough morning." Alex rummaged in his wallet and set a few crumpled bills on the counter. "Can you whip up something comforting for her? On me."

At the mention of food, Maia offered a tentative smile, but Alex caught the tension still lingering in her posture. She'd calmed down since the robbery, but those haunted edges around her eyes hadn't entirely disappeared. He wanted her to feel safe—if only for an hour.

Mr. Zhang squinted theatrically, then grinned. "Our first customer of the day is always the most important. Let's see... You strike me as a salad sort of lady, but how about something a little more adventurous?"

She gave a small laugh, stepping a fraction closer to Alex as she did so. "Sir, I'll eat anything you recommend."

Mr. Zhang's eyes twinkled with approval. "Excellent. I've got just the thing. Kung Pao chicken it is!" He shot Alex a conspiratorial wink as he disappeared into the kitchen. Pots clanged and steam hissed in the background, a comforting cacophony Alex knew by heart.

He gestured to one of the booths lining the windows. "Let's sit," he said softly to Maia. As they slipped into opposite seats, he felt more aware of her than he had any other woman in recent memory—how her eyes took in the modest interior, how she ran a hand nervously through her braids. A pang of protectiveness flared in his chest again.

"I hope you'll like this place," he told her, resting his arms on the small wooden table. "I'm biased, but the food's amazing. My parents have been running it since before I was born."

A spark of genuine interest lit Maia's gaze. "I've lived here a little while, but I never came in. I guess I always assumed it was more of a dinner spot. But the smell alone is telling me I've been missing out." She set down the menu she'd picked up. "Also… thanks for inviting me. You didn't have to, you know."

Alex shrugged. "Just returning the favor of your company." In truth, it was more than that. He wanted to make sure she was *okay*. When she looked out the window, scanning the street as though the thief might reappear any second, he frowned. "Still on edge, huh?"

She gave a sheepish nod. "Yeah. I can't help it. I keep picturing him lunging for my pocket again."

"You don't owe anyone an apology for being shaken." He leaned forward, lowering his voice to soothe her. "It's not every day you get robbed."

Her expression softened with relief. "Thank you."

"Glad I could help." He tried to stifle a grin at the sight of her shoulders relaxing, as if the atmosphere of sizzling food and clattering dishes was already doing her good. "Besides, this is a chance for me to check on you. For security's sake," he added, half-teasing. "We are running partners now, after all."

Maia's lips curved in a tentative smile. "Right—running partners."

Mr. Zhang's voice boomed from the kitchen, calling out instructions, and a waitress whisked past with a tray. Maia glanced curiously after her, studying the hustle of cooks prepping saucepans and chopping vegetables. Alex could almost feel her tension continue to dissolve.

When their waitress arrived with two steaming plates of Kung Pao chicken, rice, and a cup of tea for each, Alex watched Maia's eyes light up. She looked—dare he think it—*happy*. The morning's terror seemed distant for a moment.

"I'm so excited to try this," she admitted, scooping up a forkful of tender chicken and peppers. "I usually jog on an empty stomach, so I'm starving by now."

He chuckled. "That explains the speed of your fork. Slow down before you burn your tongue."

She grinned through her next mouthful. "This is amazing," she said once she swallowed. "The sauce, the seasoning—it's exactly the pick-me-up I needed."

For a while, they both focused on their food. Alex, too, realized he was hungrier than he'd thought. The savory food was warming him from the inside out. But not nearly as much as the unexpected relief of sharing this meal with Maia.

He found his gaze drawn to her face more than once, noticing how the tension around her eyes eased with every bite. *She's beautiful,* a quiet voice in his mind insisted, though he tried not to dwell on it. He was just checking on her, right? Ensuring her safety, that's all.

"So," he asked when she paused to take a sip of tea, "feeling any calmer?"

Maia set her cup down, exhaling slowly. "Much better, actually," she admitted. "I was worried I'd be in panic mode the rest of the day, but… this helps." Her gaze flicked to his eyes, then away, as if the intensity of meeting his stare was too much. "You help."

Alex's chest constricted in a strange, pleasant way. He cleared his throat to keep his reaction in check. "I'm glad," he murmured. "I, uh, sort of wanted to keep an eye on you anyway." He tried to sound casual, but part of him was acutely aware of the quickened beat of his own heart.

Just then, a text buzzed on Maia's phone. She glanced at it, a flicker of relief crossing her face. "My boss," she explained, locking the screen. "She's giving me some extra leeway today. Probably a mix of pity and me rarely taking sick days." She shrugged. "I'll head back soon, but at least I'm not in a rush."

"That's good," Alex replied, setting his fork down. "No point in stressing yourself out more than necessary. After all, you've been through enough."

She nodded, swirling the last of her tea. "I think I'll be okay now. Thanks, Alex… really."

"Anytime," he said, feeling that odd tug inside his chest again. A handful of other patrons, regulars by the look of them, filed into the restaurant, and Alex caught his father peeking out from the kitchen. He shot Mr. Zhang a look, silently conveying *Don't come over here.* Fortunately, his father disappeared back behind the clattering pots.

Maia sighed happily and stood, gently pushing her plate aside. "That was delicious. I owe your family's restaurant a five-star review or something." Her gaze drifted to the front doors. "But I should probably head back to work."

Alex rose with her, uncertain whether he should offer a handshake, a hug, or something else. The memory of how she'd tilted her smile at him earlier caused his heartbeat to pick up. "Alright. I'm—glad you stopped by." His words were a bit awkward, but his sincerity shone through.

Maia adjusted the strap of her bag. "I am too. This was… nice." She seemed to hesitate, as if considering what else to say. Finally, she brushed a braid off her shoulder and smiled. "See you tomorrow for our jog? Bright and early?"

He felt warmth spread through his chest. "Absolutely."

Without another word, she headed for the door, offering a quick wave. He watched her slip outside into the sunny afternoon, where a handful of passersby wandered by on their own lunch breaks. When she glanced back one last time, he couldn't contain his small, involuntary grin.

Once the door swung shut behind her, Alex eased back into his seat for a moment, heart racing in a way he hadn't felt in a long time. The day was far from over, but he already knew it wouldn't get better than this simple, unexpected lunch. After everything, Maia was safe—and maybe that meant something more than he'd dared imagine.

CHAPTER EIGHT

Maia swore the only thing powering her through the afternoon was that heaping plate of Kung Pao chicken she'd devoured earlier. By the time she ended a client call, she felt her entire body sagging with fatigue and left-over tension. Gently returning the handset to its cradle, she slumped in her office chair, elbows braced on her desk, palms pressing against her temples.

No matter how hard she tried, she couldn't shake the memory of the robbery. Every time she blinked, her mind conjured up the image of that man's hand plunging into her hoodie pocket. Even the comforting swirl of flavors from lunch —steamy rice, savory sauce—couldn't fully dislodge the memory of how she'd fallen, or of Alex sprinting to her rescue.

Focus on work, she told herself, spinning in her chair and letting the back hit the cubicle wall. Phones rang all around her as coworkers continued fielding calls and shuffling files. She'd been inundated with sympathy from her boss earlier, who encouraged her to take time off if she needed it. But with a jam-packed schedule, Maia felt obligated to stay. *I can do this. I'm strong. I'm resilient. It's just a bump in the road.*

Her gaze dropped to the ring dangling from her necklace. She closed her eyes, breathing in the stale air of her office and exhaling slowly. "I'm a fighter, I'm strong, I'm resilient," she whispered under her breath. "I will overcome whatever's affecting me because it's who I am."

She pictured a tiger bounding through a lush, green jungle—powerful, unstoppable. But after a moment, that image morphed into Alex's family restaurant, the red lanterns swaying overhead. She could practically see the steam rising from the Kung Pao chicken and remember the warmth in Alex's eyes. He'd initially rejected her as a running partner, sure, but after everything that happened, maybe she was seeing a whole new side to him. A side that might actually care.

I wonder what we'll talk about tomorrow. For a second, she allowed her pulse to steady at the thought of his presence. She definitely wanted to stick to a safer route this time, but having Alex there made the idea of jogging again feel less daunting.

A sudden ring jerked her out of her daydream. Maia snapped upright and rolled her chair closer to the desk. "Hello?" she answered, trying to sound calm.

"Mai, hey—it's me. Sorry for using your work number, but I tried your cell a few times. Are you busy?"

Aimee's voice crackled through the receiver, a thread of concern woven in.

Reflexively, Maia glanced around her cubicle for her phone. Sure enough, it sat face-down next to her laptop, missed calls lighting up the screen. *I must've been so lost in my thoughts that I didn't even notice.* "I, uh… yeah, a bit," Maia admitted, scanning the half-finished spreadsheet glaring at her from the monitor. "But I'm taking a tiny break. What's up? Everything okay?"

"It's fine here at the diner," Aimee said, her tone pitched with relief. "Rochelle mentioned you were robbed this morning, and I freaked. I told you we should've reported that creep sooner—

he had stalker vibes. Have the police found anything? Is there an update?"

Maia grimaced. The rumor mill in Sweetgum worked fast, especially with Rochelle and Mrs. Zhang fueling it. "No real updates yet. Just a vague description. I guess the police are investigating. Hopefully they'll track him down soon."

Aimee let out a little huff. "Well, I sure hope they catch him. The important thing is that you weren't hurt. Though from what I hear, you have a certain, uh, 'mystery cutie' to thank for that."

Heat prickled across Maia's cheeks. "I wouldn't call being robbed 'lucky,' but yeah, Alex was… he stepped up." She closed her eyes, recalling the adrenaline surge when she saw him chase after the thief. "Did you know he's Mrs. Zhang's son? The owners of that Chinese place on Main Street? That's how we ended up eating together."

Aimee's laugh bubbled through the receiver. "Of course I know who Mrs. Zhang is, silly. But I love that you only *just* discovered he's part of that family. So you and your hero got to have a short date—how romantic. Rochelle said you two looked pretty cozy."

Maia traced the edge of a small glass dolphin figurine perched on her desk, flushing at Aimee's teasing. "It wasn't that dreamy, trust me. We hit it off *after* some painfully awkward moments. I tried talking to him before the robbery, asked him if he'd be my running partner, and he turned me down flat." She still felt a twinge of embarrassment. "He said he was more of a solo runner."

"Wait—he rejected you?" Aimee sounded aghast. "No way."

"Yup," Maia replied, spinning her chair from side to side. "I wanted to crawl under a rock. Then, out of nowhere, the thief snatched my phone, and before I knew it, Alex was sprinting after him. He almost pinned the guy down until he wriggled free. That's how I ended up at his parents' restaurant. I guess he felt bad, or just wanted to make sure I was okay. He paid for the meal and even offered to jog with me in the future—like a bodyguard."

Aimee whistled in admiration. "Sounds like a decent guy with a hero complex—or at least a conscience. Not all men would jump into danger like that."

"True," Maia admitted, recalling the sheer determination in Alex's eyes as he dashed after the thief. "He's not big on smiling, but you can tell he's got a good heart under that aloof exterior."

"Awww, Maia," Aimee teased lightly, "it's only been one day, and you're already describing him like some lone-wolf knight in shining armor."

"Stop," Maia replied, laughing softly, though her heart gave a tiny flutter at the thought. "I'm more relieved than anything. Running again tomorrow feels less terrifying if he's there. I doubt the same robber will show up after nearly getting caught, but I don't want to take any chances."

"I get it," Aimee said, her voice softening. "And I'm glad you're not letting fear keep you from something you love."

"Honestly, if Alex hadn't offered, I probably *wouldn't* go jogging," Maia confessed, a shiver crawling up her spine at the memory. "I'm still rattled, but if he's nearby, it's a bit easier to breathe. He's... safe, somehow."

They discussed dinner plans for a few minutes, until Aimee had to return to work. After the call ended, Maia slumped forward onto her arms, letting out a long exhale. *Alex is... safe.* The notion almost made her want to laugh—he'd refused her initial invitation, then ended up saving her phone (and quite possibly her from further harm).

She mulled over her late Aunt Dianne's words: "True character shows when crisis strikes." That idea settled in her mind, making her wonder about Alex's story. Something about his eyes told her he'd seen heartbreak of his own. *Maybe that's why he ran alone*—maybe he was trying to outpace his demons, the same way she used to chase away stress with every footfall.

Her gaze drifted to a small sticky note pinned on her cubicle wall: a to-do list for Aunt Dianne's house. For a while, she'd been avoiding any heavy work there, but after what happened today, a part of her *craved* distraction. If she didn't focus on tasks—like clearing out the weeds in front of the house or organizing the boxes left in the garage—she'd only brood over the robbery.

She checked the time on her computer: 1:00 p.m. The day stretched ahead, but she reminded herself that her boss had granted her leniency. *Should I take the rest of the day off?* The idea of going home and letting her imagination run wild wasn't appealing, though. Better to stay active, keep her hands busy— perhaps by tackling some chores at Aunt Dianne's place once her shift ended.

If the streets were bustling around that neighborhood, she wouldn't be alone if she decided to do some yard work. Something about ripping out weeds—maybe in memory of her aunt, who'd always fussed over unkempt lawns—felt like a good way to reclaim her own peace.

"I can do that," she murmured, squaring her shoulders as she reached for one of the scattered files on her desk. "Small steps, right?"

Snapping out of her reverie, Maia straightened her workspace. With a renewed sense of purpose, she dove back into her spreadsheet, letting the steady rhythm of typing anchor her. She might not have all the answers about the thief, or about Alex Zhang, for that matter, but she knew she wasn't about to let fear dictate her life.

As she lost herself in numbers and data entry, a tiny flicker of excitement wormed its way through the lingering dread in her mind. *Tomorrow, bright and early,* she thought, allowing a hint of a smile at the corner of her lips. *Whatever the reason, Alex agreed to jog with me—and that means I'm not facing this alone anymore.*

GARDENING HAD NEVER BEEN her forte.

Maia stood on Aunt Dianne's creaking wooden porch late that afternoon, a massive plastic trash bag at her feet, surveying the overgrown jungle that had once been a lovingly tended yard. The porch boards groaned under her weight, reminding her that there was a lot more to fix around this house than just the plants.

Well... no time like the present, she thought, taking in a steadying breath.

She'd changed out of her work slacks and blouse in favor of stretchy black pants and a comfy sweater—clothes that allowed her free movement as she waded into the mess of tall grass and tangled weeds. Aunt Dianne used to maintain the yard meticulously until her health declined, and the contrast between that memory and the current wildness made Maia's heart clench. Georgia's soil was famously fertile, and it seemed like *everything* had decided to sprout in this neglected patch.

Bits of dead plants mixed with healthy weeds, forming a chaotic tapestry of stems and leaves. She crouched down, tugging at stray vines and brittle branches, stuffing them into her bulging plastic bag. Her mind drifted to the earlier part of the day—her near-robbery, Alex's rescue, and the strong, warm taste of the food at his parents' restaurant.

She gave the tied-off bag an experimental shake. Already filled with dead leaves, the plastic rustled ominously, on the verge of bursting. *Like the life of this home just... got thrown away,* she mused, swallowing a lump in her throat. Aunt Dianne had once created vibrant displays of flowers in color-coordinated pots, each corner of the yard a miniature art piece. Now, those same pots stood bare and hollow, arranged like solemn sentinels around the porch.

Still, Maia was determined not to let the place stay lifeless. Heading down the porch steps, she popped open her trunk, rummaging for the fertilizer, seeds, and small gardening tools she'd picked up on her way here. "I can bring back at least a fraction of what Aunt Dianne created," she whispered, hauling the supplies back up. If anything, it would keep her busy—keep her mind off *him*.

She started by sifting new soil into each pot, sneaking glances at the road every now and then. The street lay quiet, the neighboring houses drawn tight against the twilight. *No sign of suspicious strangers,* she reassured herself. And that *should* have put her at ease, but anxiety still flickered at the edges of her thoughts. *Getting robbed in broad daylight isn't exactly forgettable.*

A memory of an even harsher voice intruded: *Get over it, Maia. It's been years.* Derek's words echoed, tugging her back to a time when she'd been shattered by grief—only for him to dismiss her pain as excessive. She gritted her teeth, pressing down on the soil with more force than necessary. *Good riddance.* She'd escaped his self-centered judgments, but every once in a while, they still haunted her, popping up uninvited like the weeds she was uprooting.

Derek's shortcomings aside, he hadn't been *all* bad—he had known how to be thoughtful in small bursts. His gifts had been lavish, and he had, at least initially, displayed genuine concern for her feelings. But it was always a timer ticking down until the next dismissal, the next time he made her traumas feel like an inconvenience. Eventually, the heartbreak he caused eclipsed the material niceties he offered.

She shook off the thought, tilting a pot to examine whether it was level. *I really shouldn't be thinking about him.* Especially not here, at Aunt Dianne's place—a supposed refuge.

After carefully placing seeds in the newly potted soil, she

dusted off her hands and surveyed her progress. The sun had begun its descent without her noticing, painting the horizon orange and purple. The shifting light cast long, soft shadows across the yard. *It's getting late,* she realized, glancing at the quiet block. *I should wrap this up.*

Heading inside to grab a broom, she swept the porch briskly. Dirt skittered across the ancient wooden slats, some of it falling between the cracks. *Into the earth's hands now,* she thought, a small pang of sadness tugging at her. It felt like she was brushing away the last remnants of her aunt's presence. *But maybe Aunt Dianne would be happy I'm cleaning up, making room for something new to grow.*

Finally, she tied off the garbage bag and tossed it into a small bin near the side of the house, already imagining her next steps. She'd probably need professional help with the lawn, but at least the potted plants were a start. Her heart felt a bit lighter seeing them ready for a fresh beginning—like a promise she'd made to keep Aunt Dianne's memory alive.

I really should get going. The street looked deserted as she hauled her supplies back into her trunk, no friendly neighbors out for an evening stroll. An unsettling hush lay over the houses, the kind that made her hyperaware of how alone she was. *I'm in my car, it's fine,* she told herself. The engine roared to life, and she took one last glance at the porch—her aunt's porch—before driving off.

As she navigated the winding, lamplit roads toward home, her thoughts drifted to the next morning's run. A swirl of anticipation and nerves danced in her stomach. Alex had been so aloof at first. Would he revert to that stoic persona, uninterested in small talk, or remain the kind protector who'd chased down a thief and made sure she was okay?

I guess I'll find out, she thought, rolling down her window for a blast of cooling evening air. Part of her worried that he might get tired of this arrangement—tired of checking on her, tired of her skittishness. But the bigger part of her clung to a budding optimism. Maybe tomorrow's jog would anchor her fears and let her see more of who Alex Zhang really was.

For tonight, though, she'd settle for a long shower, some journaling, and maybe a cup of chamomile tea to chase away the ghosts of past relationships. *I'm safe now,* she reminded herself. *And no matter which version of Alex I meet tomorrow, I'm going to keep moving forward.*

THE NEXT MORNING, Maia woke before her alarm, which was almost unheard of. She'd tossed and turned all night, replaying her near-robbery and the way Alex had come through for her. By the time sunrise hinted at the edges of her curtains, she finally gave up on sleep and laced up her running shoes with a soft swirl of anticipation in her chest.

A brisk morning chill greeted her when she stepped outside, but the sky was already blushing with the promise of dawn. Normally, she would relish the stillness—a chance to untangle her thoughts alone. Today, though, she had company.

She jogged a few blocks until she reached the familiar intersection where Alex said he'd meet her. Sure enough, he was there: tall and steady, a dark hoodie zipped up against the crisp air. When he spotted her approach, he inclined his head, a small, almost shy smile curving his lips.

"Morning," he said quietly.

"Morning," Maia replied, and found herself smiling back. A ripple of nerves danced in her stomach, though she wasn't sure if it was from the chill or from him.

They set off at an easy pace, shoes tapping on asphalt in unison. The first few minutes passed in companionable silence, and Maia tried not to overthink it. Alex had a guarded vibe, and she was still figuring out how to fit into that space. Eventually, he glanced over.

"Did you get any sleep?" he asked, voice low.

She let out a rueful laugh. "Not much. Guess I had too many thoughts buzzing around."

He nodded once, his dark eyes contemplative. "Makes sense… after everything."

There was a note of empathy in his tone that took her by surprise. She wanted to press him—*Was he referring to her ordeal, or did he have his own battles keeping him awake?*—but she decided not to pry. Instead, she switched the focus.

"What about you?" she asked. "Up this early every day, or are you making a special exception?"

Alex's mouth quirked in a faint smirk. "Special exception, I guess. Needed a change of pace. Figured fresh air might help clear my head."

She eyed him, curiosity tugging at the back of her mind, but resisted the urge to push. "Well, I'm glad you did."

They fell into a steady rhythm, and Maia felt her breathing sync with his—oddly comforting. The tension she'd carried from yesterday's chaos began to loosen. At one turn, Alex slowed, eyes flicking around them warily. Maia's chest tightened with a flash of memory: the thief's hand in her pocket, the stunned terror she'd felt.

She swallowed, forcing a steady exhale. "We're safe, right?"

His gaze met hers, calm and reassuring. "Yes," he said softly. "Just being cautious."

She nodded, her pulse calming at his certainty. "I appreciate it. I feel safer with you here."

For a second, his expression softened, the guardedness in his eyes easing. "Good," he murmured.

They continued another loop, dawn giving way to morning light. By the time they returned to the intersection, Maia's muscles hummed with the pleasant burn of exertion—and a subtle warmth in her chest that had nothing to do with running.

She turned to him as they slowed to a stop, pulling her hoodie sleeves over her hands. "Thanks for coming out," she said, breathless. "I wasn't sure I'd ever feel normal running again, but this… helped."

Alex slipped his hands into his pockets, his stance casual despite the beads of sweat on his brow. "No problem." His words were short, but the sincerity behind them struck her.

"Same time tomorrow?" she asked with a hopeful smile.

He nodded, the corners of his mouth tugging upward in the faintest grin. "Sure. Tomorrow."

With that, he gave a slight wave and started down the sidewalk back the way he'd come. Maia watched him for a moment, feeling her heart thump a little harder than usual. Then she turned, heading to her own block, where her house waited.

As she walked, the world around her felt just a bit less lonely, a bit more alive. Maybe it was because for once, she hadn't jogged alone—or maybe it was the unexpected gentleness beneath Alex's guarded exterior. Either way, by the time Maia reached her front steps, her lips had curved into a soft smile. She couldn't quite say why, but she knew she was already looking forward to tomorrow.

$\mathcal{A}$lex woke even earlier than the day before. He'd never considered himself a morning person, yet here he was—checking the time anxiously, then heading out the door before dawn. A cool hush wrapped around the quiet street as he walked, breath mingling with the crisp air. *All this just to jog with a near-stranger?* he thought wryly. But the thought of Maia made that label—"stranger"—feel absurdly wrong.

By the time he reached their agreed-upon spot, the sky was still a deep indigo, just beginning to brighten at the edges. His heart kicked up when he spotted movement in the distance— Maia, jogging toward him, her braids swaying gently with each step. She wore simple black leggings and a thin hoodie tied around her waist, revealing a fitted tank top that highlighted her softly curving figure. Even in the faint light, he could appreciate the gentle glow on her deep brown skin.

She slowed to greet him, a subtle warmth in her gaze. "Morning," she said, voice carrying an undercurrent of excitement.

"Morning," Alex replied, his own voice coming out more subdued than he intended. She was so effortlessly beautiful, her features a striking blend of high cheekbones, full lips, and large, expressive eyes. He caught himself noticing the shapeliness of her hips and the confident lift of her chin. A quiet realization tugged at him—he'd rarely paid such close attention to anyone's appearance since his divorce.

"Ready?" Maia asked, adjusting the elastic holding her braids behind her head.

He nodded, tearing his focus away from the soft curve of her shoulders. "Let's do it."

They set off at a brisk pace, the rhythmic patter of sneakers echoing through the still-sleeping neighborhood. Though they ran in silence at first, it wasn't an awkward one. Alex found himself oddly comfortable beside her, matching her stride. Every so often, he'd glance in her direction, noticing how the early-morning light played across her warm complexion. She looked poised, confident—even if he sensed a tiny trace of lingering anxiety beneath it all.

"Feeling better about running after… everything?" he asked softly as they turned a corner. He couldn't quite bring himself to say "robbery."

Maia drew in a measured breath. "Yeah. Having you here definitely helps." Her tone was tinged with relief, but also a flicker of something else—gratitude, maybe even affection.

Alex offered a small nod in return, wondering if she could tell how much *he* appreciated having her around. For months, he'd been used to solitary runs, solitary work… solitary every-thing. Maia was the first person to break through that shell of solitude, even if only bit by bit.

They continued for another twenty minutes, weaving past lampposts and the occasional picket fence. At one point, Maia slowed, pressing a hand against her side. A delicate gold chain bounced against her collarbone—a ring glinting from it. Alex glanced away quickly, not wanting to stare. *A wedding ring?*

Engagement ring? The question pricked his mind, but it didn't feel like his place to ask. Not yet.

"You alright?" he asked, breath hitching slightly from the jog.

She caught his gaze, the corners of her lips curving upward. "I'm good," she assured him, pausing to stretch her calf. "Just need to catch my breath." A hint of humor sparked in her eyes. "I don't want to keel over before we make it back."

He allowed a tiny smile. "Fair enough."

They resumed at a gentler pace, eventually looping back to their starting point. Early sunshine now bathed the street, revealing more of Maia's features—her smooth brow, the subtle sheen of sweat on her temples. Alex's chest felt unexpectedly light. He opened his mouth to suggest breakfast or coffee, but Maia beat him to it.

"Wanna come by my place for a smoothie?" she asked, tucking an errant braid behind her ear. "It's not too far from here, and I promise my blender skills won't disappoint."

Part of him startled at how quickly she offered, but another part felt relieved that she wanted him around. "Sure," he managed, grateful his voice didn't crack. "Lead the way."

She grinned, and together they headed down the block. Only a few minutes later, Maia stopped in front of a modest two-story house with a little porch elevated by wooden steps. Planters brimming with cheerful marigolds lined the walkway, and the siding was painted a warm, soft gold that seemed to reflect her personality: inviting and vibrant. Alex felt the corners of his mouth lift. The place looked as friendly as she did.

"C'mon in," Maia said, bounding up the steps and unlocking the door.

Alex followed, entering a small foyer that opened into a cozy living area. The walls were painted in burnt orange and honey-yellow hues, lending the space a warm, comforting ambiance. Plush sofas in earthy browns and rust-colored throw pillows gave it a lived-in feel. There was also a polished wooden staircase leading to the second floor. The entire house smelled faintly of vanilla and something floral—maybe the remnants of a scented candle.

"Make yourself comfortable," Maia offered, walking past a small dining nook into the open kitchen. "I'll grab the fruit and such. Unless you want to help?" She cast him a playful, questioning glance.

He hesitated, drawn to how the sunlight slanted through the window, highlighting the copper undertones of her skin. "Uh, I can watch," he murmured. "I'm not exactly a whiz in the kitchen."

She laughed, opening the fridge. "Well, lucky for you, smoothies are foolproof." She pulled out a bowl of fresh blueberries, a bag of spinach, and some yogurt. "What else... bananas?"

"Sure," Alex agreed, easing onto a stool at the counter. He noticed how well-kept everything was, from the rows of spice jars to the carefully arranged kitchen towels. With each passing second, his curiosity about her grew—her habits, her daily life, the reason she wore that ring around her neck. *Patience,* he reminded himself.

He was about to ask how she was holding up after the robbery, but her phone buzzed sharply on the counter. She muttered a quick "Sorry" and snatched it up, heading into the adjacent living room for privacy. He caught a few words drifting through the open layout—something about scheduling, Sunday availability, and lawn care.

So it's a call about yard work?

As she paced back and forth, her exasperation bled into her tone. Her expression tightened whenever she paused to listen. Finally, she ended the call with a slightly forced laugh. "Alright. Thanks anyway. Bye."

Setting down her phone, Maia inhaled, trying to reset her

emotions before meeting Alex's gaze. "Sorry. Bit of a scheduling hiccup. I've been trying to find a landscaper for a big project, but nobody's free when I need them."

He leaned his forearms on the table, curiosity piqued. "A big project, huh?"

She nodded, carefully washing the blueberries. "Mmm. It's a yard in… well, let's just say it's in bad shape. Feels like half the county's gardeners are already booked solid." She patted them dry and dropped them into the blender alongside spinach and ice. "I don't mind doing some of it myself, though. Hard work never hurt anyone."

She fired up the blender, drowning out any response he might have had. Alex let his eyes roam her kitchen: shining appliances, color-coordinated oven mitts. It was *so* different from the unkempt chaos he'd left behind when he first returned to Sweetgum, back when he could barely drag himself out of bed.

The sound finally died, and Maia poured the smoothie into two tall glasses. She slid one toward Alex, a hopeful glint in her eyes.

"Moment of truth," she teased, resting her hands on the counter.

He lifted the glass for a tentative sip. Tangy sweetness and a hint of creamy spinach hit his taste buds—and it was surprisingly good. "Wow," he admitted with a satisfied nod. "You weren't kidding."

She beamed, relief visible in the slight relaxation of her shoulders. "Thanks. Told you I have my smoothie game on point."

A flicker of relief and pride danced across her face before she settled into the other chair, sipping from her own glass. It felt cozy, almost domestic, sharing a quiet moment in her kitchen. He cleared his throat, forcing himself to remember they were basically strangers. *But are we, really?* a voice in his mind countered. They'd certainly been through enough already.

His gaze drifted toward her necklace again—he couldn't help it. "So you mentioned this yard is a big task," he said, trying to push the ring question out of his mind. "If you need help, I've got free hours. Most days." He wondered if the offer sounded too forward, but something about her made him want to volunteer.

Her face lit up with a genuine smile. "Really? You'd help me mow a massive, overgrown lawn?"

"I'm probably not as good as a professional," he admitted, "but I'm decent with yard equipment. No problem."

"Wow," she breathed, stirring the straw in her smoothie. "I didn't expect that. But yes, I'd love the help."

A warm rush filled his chest at the gratitude shining in her eyes. He realized just how rarely he'd seen that look directed his way lately. "I, uh… guess I'll let you pick the time," he said, doing his best to sound casual.

"Sure," Maia said softly, then took another thoughtful sip. Her eyes met his over the rim of her glass. In that moment, Alex felt the air shift between them, a subtle, unspoken awareness that they weren't just two people jogging together out of necessity anymore.

They finished their smoothies, exchanging small talk about local shops and her daily routine. Beneath the gentle banter, Alex sensed a current of something deeper—uncertainty, hope, and maybe even attraction. His heart thrummed at the possibility that Maia might be feeling it too.

When he finally stood to leave, she followed him to the door, her cheeks flushed. "Thanks again for, uh, everything. The jog and… well, the yard offer," she said, fiddling with the chain around her neck. The sight of the ring once more triggered a pang of curiosity in him, but he forced it down. "Can we go over the details during tomorrow's jog?"

"Definitely," he said, ignoring the jolt of excitement that shot through him at the thought of seeing her again. "Just let me know when. We'll conquer that jungle together."

She laughed, the sound light and melodic. "Deal."

He gave a small nod and stepped back into the warming morning air, glancing over his shoulder to see her linger in the doorway. Her expression was warm, open—even if there was a layer of hidden sadness beneath it. And in that moment, Alex realized just how much he wanted to peel back those layers, to learn who Maia truly was.

He turned toward the sidewalk, a swirl of emotions churning in his chest. *Maybe I'm not ready. Maybe neither of us is.* But he couldn't deny the sense of calm—and a spark of something else—that filled him around her. He needed to see more of that spark, and something told him this yard project might only be the beginning.

As Alex walked away from Maia's house, he caught himself smiling like a fool. And for the first time in a long while, he didn't mind in the slightest.

CHAPTER TEN

$\mathcal{M}$aia had hardly slept. She kept thinking about Alex's easy agreement to help with her neglected yard—and replaying every moment of the previous morning's run. The natural closeness between them had been so unexpected. Now, as she tied her shoelaces for today's jog, she felt a flutter of nerves in her stomach. *Would he show up again? Would the conversation keep flowing, or revert to awkward silence?*

She stepped out into the early dawn light, inhaling the cool air. The neighborhood was peaceful, with only a few porch lights flickering like distant stars. Her short walk to the intersection where she and Alex had agreed to meet felt longer today. She half expected him not to be there, brushing off his offer to help as a polite gesture.

But there he was—a tall silhouette with broad shoulders, leaning casually against the street sign. Maia's heart gave a little leap at the sight of him, the knot of anxiety in her chest loosening. Even in the low light, she could make out his dark hair, the soft set of his mouth, and the confident stance that made her feel instantly safer.

"Morning," she called, coming to a stop.

Alex glanced up from his phone, slipping it into his hoodie pocket. "Morning." He offered a faint smile—one that Maia found more reassuring than she'd expected.

They started off at a gentle trot, feet tapping out a steady rhythm on the pavement. The sky above them was tinged with pale pink, the sun just beginning to creep over the rooftops. For a few minutes, neither spoke, but unlike before, it wasn't heavy or awkward. A comfortable hush stretched between them, as if they were easing into each other's presence for the second day in a row.

Eventually, Maia cleared her throat. "So... about the yard." She glanced sideways to gauge his reaction. "Were you serious when you said you'd help out?"

Alex nodded without missing a step. "Of course. If you still need me, I'm all in."

Surprised yet pleased, Maia slowed to a brisk walk. "You know it's a huge job, right? The lawn's basically a jungle. I've been chipping away at it for months, but it needs real muscle and a full day's work."

He gave a good-natured shrug. "I've got two arms and flexible hours. Sunday might be best. I can come by in the afternoon."

She felt a rush of gratitude, a small smile tugging at her lips. "That would be great. Five p.m., maybe? It's still light enough outside, but not scorching."

"Sounds perfect," he agreed.

They continued, picking up their pace again. Maia's heart pumped not just from the jog but from the knowledge that someone—a near stranger, at that—was genuinely willing to help her out. She couldn't shake the sense that Alex was operating on some unspoken code of decency. *Or maybe he just wants to keep an eye on me after the robbery,* she thought, still touched either way.

She quickened her steps, breath coming faster. Alex matched

her stride, his sweater rippling with each movement. Deciding they should know more about each other if they were going to be working side by side, she ventured, "So you mentioned you work from home. What do you do, exactly?"

His gaze flicked her way. "Graphic design. Mostly freelance. I manage layouts, branding, stuff like that for clients, mainly in Atlanta."

"Wow," she breathed, genuinely impressed. "That's pretty creative. I've never met anyone who freelances like that for a living."

He let out a small laugh. "Well, now you have."

They rounded a corner near a quiet park. Maia noticed the ring swinging from her necklace, a habit she'd grown so used to she barely thought about it—until she caught Alex's eyes dip toward her neck. Heat rose in her, even though she knew her dark skin rarely showed it. She slowed to a walk again, deciding the moment was right to address the curiosity she sensed in him.

"This… necklace," she said, touching the ring lightly. "I saw you eyeing it."

Alex's cheeks tensed slightly, as if embarrassed to be caught, but he didn't deny it. "I won't lie—it had me wondering. Looks like a wedding ring." He paused. "I wasn't sure if it meant you… well, that you might be married."

Maia exhaled, bracing herself for the usual twinge of pain. "It was my wedding ring," she clarified quietly. "I'm divorced. He cheated," she added, not wanting to sugarcoat it. "I know it probably sounds weird to keep wearing it, but… letting it go completely feels harder than I thought."

Alex's expression shifted. A flicker of understanding crossed his eyes, and Maia sensed an unexpected kinship there. "I get it," he said softly. "I'm… divorced too."

She raised her brow, surprised that they shared such a personal parallel. "Really?"

"Six months ago," he answered, glancing away as if the memory was still raw. "She didn't cheat, but things fell apart in a bad way. Couldn't stay together."

Maia's heart twisted with a pang of sympathy. "I'm sorry."

He waved a dismissive hand, though his voice held a note of finality. "Don't be. It was for the best."

They both lapsed into silence, letting that revelation settle between them. Maia felt a swirl of emotions—relief that he understood her complicated attachment to the ring, sorrow at the pain he must have gone through, and a spark of connection that someone else in this sleepy town shared her struggles.

They reached a small footbridge over a trickling creek that ran through the park. Maia nodded for them to stop, and they leaned on the wooden railing to catch their breath. The morning sun glinted off the water, reflecting in patches on their faces.

Maia decided to push the conversation somewhere safer, or at least less painful. "Have you heard anything from the police?" she asked, her voice still soft. The memory of her robbery attempt still clung to her, especially in the quiet moments.

Alex shook his head.

She nodded. "I called them this morning, actually. They're still investigating." She swallowed. "I admit, I kinda hope they find him. I had a nightmare last night—a replay of the whole thing."

Alex met her gaze, a flicker of compassion in his dark eyes. "Don't be ashamed. Something like that would shake anyone up. It's only been a couple of days. Take your time to recover."

Maia's chest eased at his gentle tone. "Thanks," she murmured, offering a small smile. "I appreciate that."

They lingered a moment longer, the light breeze grazing Maia's braids. She took in Alex's steady presence, his broad shoulders outlined by the sunlight. *Strange, how comfortable I feel with him,* she thought. *We barely know each other, yet... we share some big experiences.*

Alex tapped his watch. "Guess we should loop back before the day really gets started," he said lightly. "Work's calling."

"Yeah," Maia agreed, pushing off the railing. Her heart felt lighter, even though the conversation had dipped into serious territory. "Let's head back."

They retraced their path, jogging at a cooler pace. As they neared the intersection where they'd first met, Maia felt a wave of gratitude that she didn't have to face mornings in solitary dread anymore.

Alex walked her the last block toward her street, then slowed to a stop. "So… Sunday at five?" he prompted, tucking his hands into his sweater pockets.

She nodded, warmth filling her at the thought of spending another day together, even if it was just for yard work. "Sunday at five," she confirmed. "Thank you again, Alex. Really."

He gave a small shrug, but his eyes reflected sincerity. "Don't mention it. Thanks for trusting me to help."

They exchanged a brief, meaningful glance. Then, almost shyly, Alex gave her a short wave and started off in the opposite direction. Maia watched him go, her mind buzzing with equal parts curiosity and hope. *Two divorces, a robbery, and now yard work together.* It was an unconventional way to bond, but something about it felt surprisingly right.

Heading home, she couldn't help but smile to herself—her ring swaying gently from its chain, no longer feeling quite so heavy.

EVER SINCE THAT morning they shared smoothies at her house, Maia noticed a shift in her routine with Alex. By midweek, he'd insisted on meeting her outside her front door for their daily jog—and walking her right back home once they were done. The gesture both warmed and flustered her, given how guarded he'd once been. Yet every time she opened the door at dawn to find him waiting with a soft, half-smile, her heart did a little flip she couldn't quite control.

Now, Sunday had rolled around, just two days after their new habit formed. Maia's week had buzzed with deadlines at work and persistent questions swirling in her mind about the man who'd recently become part of her life. He remained polite and protective during their jogs, inquiring about her well-being at every turn, but still kept a frustratingly tight lid on his deeper thoughts. The only glimpse into his past had been that one conversation about their divorces—a moment that had felt painfully vulnerable but also surprisingly comforting.

She reminded herself that they didn't need to be best friends just because they ran together. But a part of her yearned to peel back more layers—after all, that was who she was: someone who liked truly knowing people.

And tonight, there was a chance to see a bit more of him.

"This is it," she said, gesturing to Aunt Dianne's property.

The street was quiet, the sun lowering beyond the rooftops, painting everything in a dusky gold light. Georgia's chilly autumn air settled in, promising it would get even colder once the sun fully set. Maia's car was parked in front, Alex's right behind it. She'd asked him to come at five, hoping they'd have a few hours of daylight to trim back the wild overgrowth.

Alex hit a button on his key fob, securing his car. He joined Maia by the sidewalk, eyeing the monstrous lawn of tangled weeds and knee-high grass. *More like hip-high,* Maia mused, noting how tall some patches had grown.

"Wow," he muttered, stepping carefully off the stone path and into the jungle-like vegetation. He plucked a thick strand of weed that nearly reached his hip. "We've definitely got our work cut out for us."

Hearing him say *we* stirred a little glow of gratitude in Maia's chest. Restoring Aunt Dianne's home had become her personal project, one she'd been reluctant to let anyone else share. But Alex—steady, capable Alex—had offered to help like it was the most natural thing in the world.

"Yeah, I'm not expecting we'll get everything done tonight," Maia replied as she walked to her trunk. "I figured we'd just start on the outskirts, hack down the worst parts, then call it a day." She yanked out a pair of pruning shears, followed by a second set, and handed one to Alex.

He nodded, sizing them up. "Sure. Works for me."

His direct gaze flicked to hers, and Maia felt that small flutter again—the same gentle thrill she'd come to associate with his presence. *How are you this helpful and also so reserved?* she wondered.

"Were you busy earlier?" he asked, coming to stand beside her. "We could've done this in the afternoon if that worked better."

She fit snug gardening gloves on her hands. "Well, I didn't want to hog your Sunday." A self-conscious laugh escaped her. "You offered to help, but I felt bad dragging you out here for hours on your day off."

A soft snort left him. "I'm the one who volunteered, remember? This is me repaying all those smoothies and morning runs."

Despite the fading sunlight, Maia caught his faint grin—a sight she was still getting used to. Her chest tightened pleasantly. "Right," she said, swallowing a surge of warmth. "Either way, we're here. Let's get started before we lose the rest of the light."

They waded through the tall grass, separating to tackle opposite edges of the yard. Alex moved with a surprising intensity, snipping down unruly weeds in quick, sure sweeps of his shears. Bits of grass and greenery toppled onto the sidewalk in a messy pile. Maia's progress was slower, methodical—she paused now and then to wipe her brow, already sweaty despite the cool air.

It didn't help that watching Alex was... *distracting.* Every time she glanced over, he was cutting through vines and tangled stalks like a pro. Part of her couldn't resist lingering on the flex of his forearms, the way his cap shaded his strong features, the focus etched in his dark eyes. Who was this man who could chase off robbers one day, design graphics another, and hack away weeds with ease on a Sunday night?

"Slow down over there," she teased, raising her voice to carry across the yard. "If you go too fast, you might lose a finger."

He cast her an amused look, panting lightly from exertion. "Don't worry, I've handled my share of sharp tools." He tossed a fistful of cut vines aside. "I grew up learning to use all sorts of things—kitchen knives, chainsaws, garden shears. My dad insisted on it, especially since they run a restaurant. I guess he wanted me to be self-sufficient."

"So you can cook, mow lawns, defend people from street thieves—what can't you do?" Maia teased, smiling broader than she meant to.

He chuckled, the deep sound drifting through the chilly air. "Plenty, trust me. I'm just a decent multitasker."

Maia moved a few steps closer to the old wooden fence, carefully clipping an overgrown bush. "Your parents must be proud. Owning a restaurant in a small town like Sweetgum is no small feat. Everyone raves about your family's food."

"They worked hard for it," Alex agreed. "I respect what they built, even if my path ended up going another direction."

He didn't elaborate, and Maia decided not to push. *He'll share more when he's ready.* She could sense his tension when the topic hovered too closely to personal matters—like the divorce, or why he'd come back here.

A lull settled in, the snip-snip of shears filling the space. The temperature dipped with the setting sun, and Maia could see her breath faintly in the air. Despite the chill, sweat beaded at her temples. She was grateful for Alex's help; this job would've taken her days alone.

Eventually, she paused to catch her breath, pressing gloved hands against her knees. A passing cyclist rang a small bell in greeting, glancing at the half-cleared lawn with mild curiosity. Maia waved back wearily.

Alex stopped as well, adjusting his cap. "You sure you want to keep going?" he asked, concern lacing his tone. "It's Sunday. You've got work in the morning. I don't want you dead on your feet."

Maia's pulse kicked up at his caring remark. *He might be reserved, but he's always noticing how I'm doing.* "I'm okay," she said, though her arms burned from the repetitive motion. "Besides, I don't want to leave you here alone, hacking away in the dark."

He shrugged, the corners of his mouth lifting in a half-smile. "If that's your only reason, you're free to hang back. Let me handle it."

A faint laugh escaped her. "Tempting, but I'd feel guilty. Plus, my aunt left this to me. I can't just abandon the labor to you."

The thought of Aunt Dianne warmed her. In many ways, she'd been the mother Maia lost too soon. Maia wanted so badly to honor her by restoring this place—replacing overgrown flowerbeds with new blooms and preserving the home's cheerful spirit. She just hadn't expected a near-stranger to help in such a big way.

"You've mentioned your aunt before," Alex said, stepping carefully around a patch of fallen grass. "Mind if I ask... was she the one who raised you?"

Maia's breath hitched, a gentle ache forming in her chest. She had to gather her words before responding. "Yeah. My parents passed when I was young," she confessed. "Aunt Dianne stepped in. I owe her more than I can say. Keeping this house in good shape feels like the least I can do."

She felt his gaze on her and chanced a glance back. His expression softened in empathy. "I'm sorry," he said quietly. "I know saying that doesn't fix anything, but... yeah. I can't imagine."

Her heart squeezed, both in sadness and appreciation for his genuine tone. "Thank you. It's been a long time, and I had plenty of love from Aunt Dianne. I promise, I turned out okay," she added with a small smile. "Anyway, enough about me. We should probably call it quits soon before we can't see what we're trimming."

Alex gave a small nod, assessing the sky. The horizon glowed with purple dusk, and the temperature was dropping fast. "Agreed. Let's do a bit more, then wrap up."

They continued to work in tandem for another fifteen minutes, stacking the cut weeds to one side. Maia's muscles ached by the time they finished, but a sense of accomplishment sparked in her chest. *It's a start,* she thought, surveying the now half-tamed yard.

She lifted her gloves to her face, blowing warm air onto her chilled fingers. Alex came to stand next to her, shears slung over one shoulder. A jolt of attraction shimmered through her at how he loomed, protective and strong, even now.

"I can clean up inside a bit," she offered, nodding at the house. "If you want to call it a day, I totally understand. This was more work than I expected."

"It's fine," Alex said, voice husky with fatigue. "Go ahead. I'll load these weeds into bags. Then we can head out together."

Her breath caught at *together.* The word comforted her more than she wanted to admit. "Thank you," she murmured, letting her gaze linger on his for a second before picking up her spare tools and heading toward the porch.

As she moved inside, the thought struck her again: *When*

Alex is around, everything feels... easier. She tried not to read too much into that. Maybe he was just a good guy helping a neighbor in need. Maybe. But the quickening of her heart said otherwise.

He's not just nice; he's unexpectedly sweet. And I like that a lot, she admitted to herself as she vanished into the dimly lit hallway.

And in the quiet evening air, as Alex bundled stray clumps of weeds for disposal, he found himself smiling over the simple fact that he'd spent Sunday evening shoulder-to-shoulder with Maia—braving the chill, sharing the workload, forging another small step toward something that felt suspiciously like a genuine connection.

CHAPTER ELEVEN

*W*arm steam from his coffee curled around Alex's face, leaving small droplets on his upper lip. He couldn't help but think about the previous day. They'd barely spent a few hours tending Aunt Dianne's lawn, yet Alex felt something big shifting in him every time he saw Maia. Her presence had become… comforting.

No, if he was being honest, it was more than just comfort. It was attraction—pure and simple. He liked talking to her, liked that she could be open about her past hurts. He liked the way she lit up when she talked about something she was passionate about, and how she kept pushing forward despite the weight of her divorce and losing her parents at a young age.

In short, *he liked her.*

Point blank.

He took another careful sip of his coffee, then set it down to cool beside his laptop. On the floor near his feet, Odie sprawled with a small rubber ball between his paws. The dog had learned to toss it in the air and catch it, a handy trick for when Alex was knee-deep in work emails.

Today was no exception. Alex glanced at the screen, scanning through his latest message from a major client. He'd delivered a big design the night before, only to receive a slew of modification requests and questions. *Great,* he thought wryly. Communicating through email threads was cumbersome, but he couldn't meet them face-to-face until he got the green light. He rubbed his temples, feeling a faint thread of overwhelm tug at him.

His mind drifted back to Maia again. *Yesterday was so... easy.* Sure, they'd spent much of it chopping down stubborn weeds and tall grass, but there'd been a pleasant hum beneath it all—a sense that he wasn't alone in his tasks for once. By the time she reemerged from the house, he'd nearly fired up the lawn mower, hoping to make a bit more headway. She'd insisted he leave the heavy cutting for tonight, which gave him another reason to see her. He certainly didn't mind that.

With his thoughts drifting, Alex forced himself back to the email, typing a short inquiry about scheduling an in-person meeting. After hitting *send*, he glanced at the clock. *Almost noon.* He sighed, sipping his coffee again. Maia and he had jogged earlier in the morning, as had become their custom. She'd seemed content with his quiet presence—she never pushed him to open up, yet there was a gentle curiosity in the way she'd glance his way now and then. He liked her patience, how she didn't hound him with personal questions or try to fill every silence with chatter.

Still, he wanted to ask her so many things. Did she ever consider taking off that wedding ring she wore on a chain? Did she suspect her ex might have lingering feelings after cheating on her? The very thought made Alex bristle. *Who cheats on someone like Maia?* The idea felt absurd. She exuded warmth and kindness. She was beautiful, too—unapologetically so, with a quiet confidence that pulled people in. *She's exactly the kind of person you'd hold onto,* he mused, not sabotage.

"Life gets complicated," he whispered. *Maybe I'm just naive.*

He tapped his fingers lightly on the table, noticing Odie's ears perk at the sound. Alex paused to scratch him behind the ear, earning a contented huff.

He let his gaze trail back to his laptop, thoughts migrating to what lay ahead: finishing the lawn tonight, maybe helping with more tasks around Aunt Dianne's place if Maia would let him. *Does she plan on living there?* he wondered. She'd only said it belonged to her aunt, but not much more. Yet the house had this cozy, lived-in vibe, even in its current state of disrepair.

He reached for his coffee again, swirling the liquid before sipping. *I want to know more.* Something about Maia had always intrigued him, even when he'd first caught sight of her running at dawn. Each detail she revealed—her family's story, her divorce, her resilience—only made him want to dig deeper. *She's an enigma, and I want to solve her.*

His fingers hovered over his keyboard, but he couldn't focus on another design. The memory of Maia's smile drifted to the forefront of his mind again. She might have lost her parents and gone through a painful heartbreak, but she carried herself with grace, determination, and a lively spark that made him want to be near her. It was a spark he recognized in himself—one he'd tried to bury after his own divorce. He caught glimpses of it every time they talked, and it ignited something in him he thought he'd lost.

Stop overthinking, he told himself, but that was easier said than done. He clicked around, opening a half-finished layout for another client, but his focus wavered. *Tonight, after I help with the mowing, I'll see if she needs anything else.* Maybe they'd share a conversation that went beyond yard work or running or even their divorces—a conversation that edged into the territory of *us.*

A soft thump drew his attention—Odie had nudged his ball closer to Alex's foot, tail wagging. *Time to play, buddy?* Alex let out a small chuckle, grateful for the loyal interruption. He took another sip of coffee, then closed his design software. His creative energy was too scattered, and he wasn't the type to force it. *Meeting Maia again tonight should help clear my head.*

Setting his mug aside, Alex stood, gave Odie an affectionate pat on the head, and thought one more time of Maia. The timid excitement inside him stirred once more—excitement at the prospect of learning more about her, understanding where she came from, and seeing that gorgeous smile firsthand. He wasn't sure how deep their connection could go or what it meant in the long run. But for the first time in a very long time, he felt open to the possibilities.

And that was something he welcomed wholeheartedly.

"I CAN'T THANK YOU ENOUGH." Maia handed Alex a glass of apple juice later that night, after they'd wrapped up another round of chores at Aunt Dianne's house.

Alex leaned on the kitchen counter, taking in the cozy, slightly old-fashioned room. The fridge and toaster reminded him of the appliances his parents had owned years ago—the kind that never seemed to break. "It's really no problem," he said, sipping from the glass and letting the cool sweetness wash over him.

He'd finished mowing the lawn—a task Maia had tried to help with, until he'd insisted she head inside to work on what she called *final touches*. She seemed both flustered and thrilled by his eagerness to shoulder the heavy part of the yard work.

Now, standing here in the warm glow of the overhead light, Alex couldn't take his eyes off the woman who stood across from him. ***She looks radiant—even when she's exhausted.*

"You remind me of Superman." Maia laughed softly, propping herself on the counter beside him. "Between fending off robbers and tackling my yard, I'm starting to question whether you're actually human."

Alex felt his grin forming before he could stop it. "Superman, huh? Well, if you hadn't stopped me the other day, I would've finished mowing then." He winked, and her eyes lit up in response.

"I really appreciate it." She sighed, glancing into her half-empty glass. "I wish there was some way I could repay you."

He swirled the apple juice in his cup. "I'm happy to lend a hand—really."

Even as he said the words, a nagging question tugged at the back of his mind. *Why am I so eager?* He'd never been one to jump at requests, no matter how nice the person was. Yet with Maia, he found himself volunteering for every little chore she mentioned. It seemed the more time he spent with her, the more time he *wanted* to spend with her.

"I guess that makes you a saint," Maia teased, setting down her glass. "Being my morning guard and my evening lawn-care hero. I don't know anyone else who'd do so much for a person they just met."

A flicker of self-consciousness crept in, and Alex focused on a small table across the room—an old-fashioned wooden piece decorated with porcelain figurines. "Trust me, Maia. I'm no saint," he said quietly.

A brief silence settled in. Maia shifted, fidgeting with the hem of her T-shirt. Alex had noticed her habit of twisting fabric when she was anxious or deep in thought. He wanted to reassure her, but he wasn't sure how. *We've only known each other a couple of weeks, but I can already read her moods.*

"If there's anything else you need," he offered, "just say the word. I'm not exactly loaded with social plans, so…"

The corner of Maia's mouth quirked in a half-smile. "I appreciate that, but I think I've dragged you into enough heavy lifting already. There's just a little more inside, and then I'll be done." She paused, eyes drifting over the chipped paint along the doorframe. "Hopefully, I'll also be done feeling guilty for neglecting her home."

The admission tugged at Alex's heart. He wanted to ask more about Aunt Dianne—what she was like, how Maia came to inherit the place—but he held back, remembering how she'd briefly mentioned her aunt filling an emotional void left by her parents' passing. When Maia lifted her gaze to him, there was a trace of sadness behind her dark brown eyes.

"Were you raised here?" he asked gently.

She lowered her head, fiddling with her glass. "Yes and no. I mainly grew up in Savannah with a family friend, but Aunt Dianne was the one I leaned on when I needed support. I spent summers here sometimes." A short laugh escaped her. "I cried on her shoulder a lot, especially when life got too big."

Alex's chest tightened at the thought of her tears—he couldn't picture the vibrant, warm Maia he knew dissolving in sorrow. She caught his expression and shrugged, as if to say *that was then.*

"It's good you had her," he offered. "Everyone needs someone to confide in."

She drew a breath, flashing a more playful look. "Yeah, I guess so. How about you? Did you confide in your dad or mom? Or maybe you had a friend who listened to all your high school drama?"

Alex huffed a soft laugh, remembering how his folks would fuss over him whenever he brought home a mediocre grade or struggled with a social dilemma. "Actually, my parents were pretty easy to talk to. But I was never too needy, emotionally, I guess."

"Is that still true?" Maia pressed, curiosity brightening her eyes. "Even now—after your divorce, you didn't need someone to cry to?"

The question cut right to the core, stirring an ache inside

him. He shrugged, looking down at his shoes and noticing bits of grass clinging to them. "I opened up to my parents," he admitted, "mainly because my mom insisted on details. She's pretty passionate." A bitter flash of memory flared as he recalled how vehemently his mom had sided against Phoebe.

"But you didn't cry?" Maia asked, her tone more of astonishment than accusation.

Alex hesitated. "No," he answered simply. "I felt broken, sure, but tears never came. I was more focused on making sure I didn't lose my shares in the restaurant."

Maia's eyes clouded with concern. "Your ex tried to take that from you, too?"

He nodded, tension pricking across his shoulders at the recollection. "Yeah. I guess that worry overshadowed everything else."

Before Maia could respond, her phone buzzed. She glanced at the screen and apologized before stepping out of the room to take the call. *Probably time to wrap up,* Alex told himself, draining the last of his juice. He felt the usual tug of regret whenever their conversations ended—like they were building something real between them, and it kept getting cut short.

LATER THAT EVENING, Alex returned to his parents' place for dinner—*as usual.* The second he settled into the chair, chopsticks in hand, his mother was in full interrogation mode.

"So," Mrs. Zhang said in a sing-song voice, "you run with her, talk about your problems, and now help fix up her dead aunt's house. Why don't you just admit you love her and call her your new wife?"

Alex almost choked on his rice, while his father nearly fell off his chair laughing. "Mom, come on," Alex managed, pressing a palm to his forehead. His mother did this every time he mentioned Maia—as though she couldn't fathom any man going to such lengths without wanting marriage.

His mother set the gravy pan on the stove and came back, taking her seat. "I'm just saying, you obviously like this girl. You never do manual labor, especially not for free."

"You do hate manual labor, son," his father chimed in with an amused nod. "And you limp in here every night lately from all that yard work. Let's face it: you like her."

A wave of exasperation and something else—maybe guilt or longing—washed over Alex. "It's not… I mean, I *do* like Maia, but not—" He paused, floundering for the right words. "It's complicated, and I'm still not over Phoebe. Besides, I'm insanely busy with work."

"Oh yes," Mrs. Zhang said, eyebrows arching. "The big project requiring you to head to Atlanta soon, right? So you won't be around to be her morning bodyguard."

Alex stiffened. "You're right." He set his chopsticks down, dread swirling in his gut. *Maia's counting on me for those runs, especially after the robbery.* "I should've told her."

His father waved a hand dismissively. "Just call her after dinner, let her know."

"I would," Alex groaned, "but I don't have her number." The admission sounded ridiculous even to him. *We've spent so much time together, yet we never exchanged numbers?*

His mother's mouth fell open. "You've been seeing this woman every day for weeks now, and you don't have her number?" She shook her head, looking scandalized. "Young people these days—aren't you always texting? How on earth are you two not in constant communication?"

His father roared with laughter, wiping tears from his eyes. Alex felt the heat of embarrassment crawling up his neck.

"It's not that simple," he mumbled, picking at his rice. "We just… never brought it up. And now I'm leaving early tomorrow."

Mrs. Zhang tutted. "Then go see her tonight. Let her know, or you'll vanish to Atlanta without warning. She'll think you ditched her."

Alex's chest clamped at the thought of Maia waking up, expecting him outside her door, only to find no one there. "I guess I could swing by after dinner," he said. The mere idea sent a small jolt of excitement through him. He'd never visited her that late. *Would she even be home?*

"There you go," his dad said, satisfied. "Now, can we talk about when you're coming to help your poor old folks at the restaurant again?"

Alex laughed, letting the conversation shift to his parents' business needs. Yet Maia stayed at the forefront of his mind, the anxiety building as he realized how he might look if he just showed up out of nowhere.

Sure enough, by the time he left his parents' place, it was already past nine. He pulled up outside Maia's house, only to find the windows dark. Her car was out front, so she had to be in there—but was she asleep, or still out with her friend?

After a moment of deliberation, he rummaged in his glove compartment for a small notepad and pen, scribbling a quick message:

> Maia—
> I have to leave early for Atlanta. Big work project. Sorry I can't jog with you for a few days. I'll be back soon—let's pick up where we left off.
> —Alex

He folded the note, pocketed it, and strode up the walkway. A cold gust of wind swept across his face. He knelt, carefully sliding the paper beneath the welcome mat, making sure a corner peeked out so she'd see it. *Hopefully she checks here,* he thought, glancing at the silent house. He felt a pang of disappointment that he wouldn't see her tonight, but *at least she won't be left in the dark.*

With that, Alex hurried back to his car, started the engine, and drove off into the chilly Sweetgum night. The house lights remained dim in his rearview mirror. Though he couldn't say when he'd see her next, he prayed she'd understand—and that maybe, just maybe, she'd miss him half as much as he was starting to miss her.

CHAPTER TWELVE

It had become a ritual for Maia to stretch outside her
house before jogging each morning. She'd step onto
the porch, breathe in the fresh, slightly muggy Georgia air, and
roll her shoulders to loosen any tension lingering from yesterday's stress. Usually, she liked the quiet hush of dawn—the time
when all of Sweetgum still slept and she could have the sidewalks mostly to herself.

But today, her routine felt off.

Where is he? she muttered under her breath, scanning the
street. A breeze rustled the lush summer greenery lining the
curbs, sending a few stray leaves dancing across the asphalt. For
the past week, Alex had shown up at her front step, ready to jog
by her side. She'd grown comforted by his presence, counted on
it, even. Now, she waited, biting her bottom lip, checking the
time on her phone.

Five more minutes, she told herself, inwardly hoping he'd
round the corner any second, hoodie framing that ever-serious
face.

But ten minutes crawled by with no sign of him.

Her heart sank. She wrapped her arms around her torso

and tried to steady her breath. *This is silly—I can jog alone. He's not obligated to be here.* A persistent knot of anxiety still twisted in her stomach, though, reminding her of the fear she'd felt not so long ago about running by herself. Alex had been her comfort, her "bodyguard," and now he was suddenly… gone.

Eventually, she couldn't wait any longer. Work demanded her schedule keep moving. She pressed a hand against her sternum, inhaling sharply, and took off at a slow jog, each footfall echoing with questions pounding in her head:

Did something happen to him? Did I say something to push him away?

A spike of panic gnawed at her. *If only we'd exchanged numbers,* she thought bitterly. She picked up her pace, hoping physical exertion would chase away the unease burning in her chest.

She was barely ten minutes into her run when her phone buzzed through her headphones. Her heart leapt, foolish hope surging that maybe, *somehow,* Alex had tracked down her number. She nearly tripped in her hurry to pause her music and answer.

"Hello?" she asked breathlessly, adrenaline spiking.

"Well, that's a voice I've been hoping to hear."

Her stomach plummeted at the slick tone she recognized all too well. *Derek.* A freezing wave of dread pushed aside the flicker of excitement she'd felt only seconds ago.

"Derek?" she managed, her throat tightening.

He gave a low chuckle. "You changed your tune awfully quick. But hey, can't a guy call to see how you've been?"

Maia's pulse hammered; she stopped dead in her tracks, the summer breeze doing nothing to soothe the sudden cold that prickled over her skin. "Derek, why are you calling me?" she demanded, forcing her voice not to waver.

"Why wouldn't I?" he replied smoothly. "After all we shared, I'd think you'd at least—"

"I'm not your anything," Maia cut him off, voice trembling with fury. The old instincts roared back: the reflex to manage Derek's feelings, to calm him, to avoid conflict at all costs. *No.* She wouldn't revert to that. Not now, not ever again.

Silence stretched over the line until Derek's voice turned dark. "You're being petty."

Heat flooded Maia's cheeks. She clenched her free hand into a fist, bile rising at his audacity. "I'm being real," she hissed, anger burning in her chest. "You don't get to call me like nothing happened, like you didn't treat me like dirt and then blame me for your own mistakes."

For a split second, no sound came from the other end. Then he spat, "You're a real bitch."

Her hand shook. She jerked the phone away from her ear, something vicious in her wanting to fling it onto the pavement. With a fierce shake of her head, she steeled herself and pressed end—cutting him off mid-rant.

Her lungs felt constricted, tears pricking her eyes. She stared at the phone for a heartbeat before blocking his number outright. *Never again,* she vowed silently.

She inhaled shakily, wiping away the angry tears that had gathered. *It'll take more than a phone call to ruin my day,* she tried to reassure herself, ignoring how hollow the words felt.

Yet deep down, she couldn't deny Derek's reappearance had rattled her.

By the time Maia slogged through two long work meetings, put out four small office crises, and dealt with three colleagues who seemed bent on testing her patience, her nerves were frayed. She slumped in her cubicle, staring blankly at a spreadsheet she was supposed to finalize.

All she could think about was how she hadn't seen or heard from Alex. *He wouldn't just vanish unless something important came up, right?*

At least she'd managed her morning jog on her own, despite the lingering fear—and Derek's call. She'd even visited the police station briefly, still hearing nothing new about the robber who attacked her. She'd resisted the urge to mention Derek's call, telling herself it was a one-off. That it couldn't count as harassment. Not yet.

"But why, Alex?" she whispered, staring at the ring dangling from her necklace. She caught herself fiddling with it again—an old nervous habit tied to memories she wished she could bury.

A brisk knock on her cubicle wall startled her. "Mrs. George," Maia greeted, quickly straightening.

The older woman, sporting neat gray locs and a pleasantly concerned expression, stepped inside. "Maia, dear, I'm here to check on you. Word around the office is you've been a bit spaced out since the robbery. Some coworkers say your productivity's dipped."

A jolt of alarm sped through Maia's chest. "I— I'm fine," she replied, voice catching slightly. She hated the idea that her personal turmoil was showing through. She'd been so determined to keep it separate this time.

Mrs. George tapped her manicured fingernails on the edge of the desk. "I'm concerned. We're a company that values mental health, remember? We can't have one of our key players falling apart because they're pushing themselves too hard."

Maia's stomach twisted. *Falling apart?*

"I'm not—I mean, I'm handling it," she stammered, forcing a wavering smile.

"We're strongly suggesting you take tomorrow off," Mrs.

George said, voice dropping to a note of empathy. "If you don't, and we see further decline, we'll have to enforce mandatory leave. Trust me, it's not a punishment—just a precaution."

It landed like a gut punch. The fear of losing her job—like what nearly happened in her days with Derek—roared to life. She cleared her throat, nodding stiffly. "I understand," she murmured. *I can't afford to slip up again.*

Mrs. George gave her hand a brief pat and departed, leaving Maia feeling drained and humiliated. She stared at the spreadsheet, mind anywhere but work. *Between Derek's call and Alex's sudden disappearance, I've let my head wander too far.* She vowed she'd push it all aside tomorrow, keep her job safe.

THAT EVENING, she found herself curled on the couch at Aimee's place, attempting to watch some random movie sequel. Aimee nursed a glass of sparkling wine, ranting about how the plot made no sense. Maia tried to focus on the flickering images, but her thoughts kept drifting to the morning: Alex's absence, Derek's call, Mrs. George's threat. She felt like she was drowning in questions, each one tugging her deeper.

"Mai?" Aimee abruptly muted the TV. "You've been a zombie since you walked in. Spill. I'm your best friend, and I'm not above prying."

Maia gave a half-hearted laugh, shifting her socked feet beneath her. "It's... complicated." She sighed. *She didn't want to bring up Derek.* Instead, she settled on the other matter plaguing her. "It's Alex."

Aimee's face melted into concern. "Did he do something? Did his big, manly ego get bruised?" She gestured wildly, already spinning the worst scenario in her head. "I thought he was sweet! The guy mowed Aunt Dianne's lawn and saved you from a mugger—where's the red flag in that?"

"No, no," Maia rushed to assure her, placing a calming hand on her friend's arm. "He's not like that at all. He's thoughtful and, I don't know, *golden*. But…" She chewed her lip. "He didn't show up for our morning jog. I waited, and waited, and he just… never came."

Aimee tilted her head. "That's it? He didn't show up once?" She snorted. "People oversleep. People get sick."

Maia groaned, hugging a cushion to her chest. "You don't understand. He never said anything. He could've stopped by later, left a note, I don't know—something. But he didn't. And I can't help thinking I did something to push him away."

"Don't you guys text?" Aimee asked, her brow furrowing. "Wait—no. You said you never swapped numbers?" She tsked. "That's the real problem. Communication meltdown."

Maia slumped further into the couch. "That's exactly it. And now my head is spinning with worst-case scenarios. What if I offended him somehow, or he's changed his mind about seeing me, or—"

Aimee pressed a firm hand on Maia's knee. "Stop. You're spiraling, and it's turning you into a version of yourself you said you'd never be again—the insecure version Derek nurtured." Her voice gentled. "I love you, but you need to breathe. Deeply. Now."

Rolling her eyes but grateful, Maia followed her friend's cue, inhaling deeply and exhaling slowly. After a few breaths, her chest loosened.

"Better?" Aimee inquired, arching a brow.

"Mildly," Maia admitted, a weak grin touching her lips.

Aimee patted her shoulder. "Look, maybe Alex is just busy or traveling for work. Maybe he has a family emergency. He'll surface when he can. Besides, you're not even sure you want anything beyond friendship, right?"

Maia opened her mouth, hesitating. "I mean… She paused, a swirl of confusion coursing through her. *I do like him, but I'm also scared to want anything more.* Derek's call had reminded her how easily life could be derailed by trusting the wrong person. "I guess I'm just used to him being there. And when he wasn't…" She shrugged helplessly, words failing her.

Aimee's gaze softened. "You've had a tough day. Let's not write him off yet, okay? And don't let Mrs. George scare you. One day of mental break might do you good."

Maia forced a small laugh, though her chest still felt tight. "I hope so. Because if I can't pull it together, I might lose everything I've been working for." She thought about Aunt Dianne's house, her job, the fragile peace she'd started to feel thanks to Alex's presence.

Aimee gave her a tight squeeze. "Hey, no doomsday predictions. Alex will probably show up tomorrow with an excellent reason, and you'll feel silly for stressing." She eyed the screen. **"Now let's unmute this bad movie. You and I have some popcorn to finish."

Maia let her head rest against the couch, trying to push away the gnawing sense of betrayal from Derek's call and the sting of Alex's sudden absence. *I'm not about to chase someone, not again,* she told herself. *If Alex is gone for good, then that's his choice. I won't become the desperate girl I used to be.*

But as the muted TV came back to life, Maia's mind drifted to the sweet smile Alex sometimes let slip—warm enough to melt away her fears. She closed her eyes, wishing that tomorrow might bring a chance to clear up this painful confusion and give her mind, and heart, a little peace.

CHAPTER THIRTEEN

Alex signaled Garrett to stop when the wine glass in his hand was filled to the brim—a generous pour he might normally have declined.

Tonight, however, he told himself he might actually enjoy it.

They stood together on Garrett's high-rise terrace, the wind ruffling the thick sweater Alex wore as he gazed at the city stretched out below. From dozens of floors up, the lights glimmered in endless patterns against the night sky, painting the urban sprawl in vibrant splotches. It was a striking sight, but Alex felt his heart tugging toward quieter horizons—toward Sweetgum and its simpler, slower pace.

"It's incredible how just one face-to-face meeting can change so much," Alex mused, sipping from his glass and savoring the fruity warmth that spread through his chest.

Garrett leaned against the railing, taking a direct swig from his bottle of red wine. The man never bothered with a glass when at home, especially after a long day teaching. "Yup," he agreed, licking his lips. "Which is why I always tell my students technology's just a tool. Nothing beats good old human connection—or the human mind." He paused to breathe in the crisp night air, letting out a contented sigh.

Alex snorted, picturing Garrett delivering a lecture to a sea of disinterested twenty-somethings. "You must sound like an old fossil, preaching that to undergrads who live on their phones."

Below them, traffic inched along congested roads. Horns honked in bursts, reminding Alex of the hustle he used to find so thrilling back when he lived here. Now, that frenetic bustle only made him long for the calm of Sweetgum—a place he'd once considered too small to contain his ambitions.

"I've never felt more ancient," Garrett admitted, "but honestly, it's also refreshing. Reminds me to keep up or get left behind." He chuckled and took another pull from the wine bottle. "Last time I talked to you, you were a complete mess, though as messy as Alex Zhang can ever seem. So... care to tell me how you pulled it off?"

Alex arched a brow. "Pulled what off?"

A few sirens wailed in the distance, and a gust of wind rattled the potted plants Garrett kept along the terrace floor. Vines wrapped around the steel railing, adding a spot of green to the concrete jungle around them.

"Getting over someone who purposefully tried to wreck you in divorce?" Garrett clarified, shooting Alex a pointed look.

"Oh..." Alex let out a low exhale, lifting his gaze to the cold stars above. "Garrett, there's no magic fix. And I'm not going to pretend I'm completely over her, because I'm not."

Garrett cocked his head sideways, swirling the bottle in his hand. "Then why aren't you fuming about how she tried to screw you over? You couldn't hold your rage in last time we met."

"It's been a long day of endless meetings," Alex replied, wearing a tired smile. "I've been distracted."

"So the secret is drowning yourself in work?"

"Not exactly." Alex's gaze flickered to the leafy vine climbing the railing. "I think about her sometimes, but… I guess I've been filling my time with other things. Leaning on my family more, focusing on helping other people. Turns out I'm not quite as isolated as I thought."

He paused, recalling quiet evenings in Sweetgum, plus the satisfaction of pulling weeds from Aunt Dianne's yard, side by side with Maia. *Her face bright when she saw the progress.* He couldn't help but wonder if she'd found his note. That single thought stirred an unexpected warmth in his chest.

Garrett stroked his neatly trimmed beard, the navy-blue durag on his head shifting slightly. "That's good. You needed a healthier outlet." He took another swig of wine, eyeing the label with the skepticism of a connoisseur. "I heard Phoebe's living it up, by the way. My sources say she threw a lavish party last week."

Alex closed his eyes for a second. "Bought another new car?" he asked dryly.

"You know it," Garrett confirmed. "She's apparently unstoppable. The rumor is she's moved on, big-time."

"Are you trying to erase all my progress or what?" Alex retorted, though without the sting of true anger. He'd known from the start that Phoebe was fearless about parading her successes, no matter how she'd gained them.

Garrett cackled. "If she's thriving, good for her. It's been almost a year, man."

"Nearly an entire year," Alex repeated in his mind. *And yet here I am, still stifled by the memory. Still occasionally grappling with bitterness.* But each day, that bitterness chipped away a little more—sometimes because of a certain woman in Sweetgum.

"Exactly," Garrett pressed, lifting the wine bottle in a mock salute. "So you can't keep wallowing. Have you talked to anyone else? Or is your heart locked away for good?"

Alex shrugged. "I've been talking to someone," he admitted,

speaking carefully, "but it's nothing serious. We just... run together, chat. I don't expect anything to come of it."

"Wait, so you're... denying yourself potential happiness because you're too scared to see where it leads?" He took a big gulp, brandishing the bottle at Alex. "Bro, do you want to be miserable forever?"

Alex gave a helpless laugh. "Can we not do this tonight? What about you, huh? You opened up the Pandora's box that is Phoebe, so it's only fair we talk Amanda next."

"She didn't leave me," Garrett grumbled, but his posture slumped. "I left her."

Alex's voice turned wry. "Because she confessed to liking someone else. If she was about to break up with you anyway, that's basically her leaving—just in a roundabout way. Not to rub salt in your wound."

He smirked lightly when Garrett scoffed, but the moment softened as they stepped back inside, escaping the city's chill. Warmth enveloped them in the living room, contrasting the night air outside.

"Okay, fine," Garrett said, continuing. "Unlike you, I've moved on."

"Is that right?" Alex teased, shutting the sliding door. "So you have an actual story to share?"

Garrett nodded, pointing the bottle at him. "I do. I met someone new—a lecturer at the university. We hit it off during the Halloween staff party. We've been on a few dates already."

Alex let out an impressed whistle. "You sly dog. Does the head of staff know, or is this a hush-hush situation?"

"Ha!" Garrett laughed, setting the wine bottle down on the kitchen island. "Nobody cares about that. Academics are ironically chill about personal relationships."

They moved into the living room, where Garrett flopped into an armchair and stared pointedly at Alex. "Now, back to this girl you've been talking to."

Alex groaned, dropping onto the sofa. "You're like a dog on a bone, man."

"Call me curious." Garrett folded his arms, eyes sparkling with mischief. "Let's hear it."

"Fine." Alex glanced at the modern chandelier overhead, tracing the angles of its metal arms. "Her name's Maia. I met her while jogging. She asked if we could be jogging partners since we kept bumping into each other, and I initially told her no."

Garrett's mouth fell open. "What do you mean, *no*? She gave you an opening, and you rejected her? I swear, Alex, you sabotage yourself."

"Let me finish." Alex let out a weary chuckle. "I wasn't ready to let someone in. But then she got robbed—"

"Whoa, that took a turn." Garrett leaned forward, eyes wide. "How on earth is that better?"

"It's not," Alex corrected swiftly. "But she was robbed while I happened to be there, so I chased down the thief and saved her phone. Afterward, I felt responsible, like I should protect her. I offered to run with her, help her out. We got closer, ended up at her house, did some chores... She's remarkable, man."

Garrett's face lit up. "And all of this in just a week or so?" He shook his head in amazement. "You work fast, whether you realize it or not."

Alex exhaled, thinking about Maia's luminous smile, the way she'd bite her lip when uncertain, or how her braids caught the sunlight whenever they jogged. "She's lost a lot—her parents, her aunt. She's divorced. Wears her wedding ring on a necklace." He rubbed at the back of his neck. "Yet she's strong. She does her own yard work, tries not to ask for help... even though she clearly needs it sometimes. I guess I admire her independence."

He paused, a slight smile tugging at his lips. "I find myself wanting to know more—like, way more. But I'm not sure if I'm ready for anything serious, or if she'd even want that from me. Right now, it's just… talking and helping."

Garrett leaned in, resting an elbow on his knee. "Sounds like you're already sweet on her. Ever think of asking her out? Or do you plan on stalling until she finds some other guy who does take that step?"

A flutter of panic seized Alex's chest. "It's not that simple. I'm nowhere near healed, Garrett." He gave a short laugh. "I've literally been acting as her bodyguard, and then I left for Atlanta without telling her. I left a note, but we never exchanged numbers. I might've already blown things."

Garrett shook his head, rummaging around in the fridge for a bag of chips. "You're killing me, man. How do you forget something as basic as exchanging numbers?"

"I know," Alex groaned, feeling the familiar shame twist in his gut. "I had to drive up here for an important work meeting, and my mind was all over the place. This morning, I kept thinking she might freak out if she goes outside expecting me and I'm not there. She's been through a robbery, so it's a jerk move on my part."

"You should've done better, but hey—if she's as sweet as you say, she might understand once you explain. Provided you do it quickly," Garrett pointed out, settling back into the armchair. "Don't wait till you get back from Atlanta to contact her. Try emailing or calling the parents' restaurant or—"

"I… might do that," Alex muttered, taking the bag of chips Garrett offered. "I just don't want to come off as some creep who hunts her down. But I guess being a little pushy is better than letting her think I'm gone for good."

He took a handful of chips, chewing thoughtfully. *All I know is that I miss her already.* It was a startling revelation, one that made his stomach flip. *Stop it, Alex,* he chided himself. *You're not that guy. Not yet. But maybe one day…*

Phoebe's betrayal still throbbed like a half-healed wound,

but Maia was different, as bright and steady as the morning sun. Maybe it was time Alex let someone shine a little light into the shadows he'd been dragging around.

"Anyway," Alex said aloud, wiping the salt from his fingers. "For now, I'll try to finalize my on-site work tomorrow, then I can get back as soon as possible." He allowed a faint grin. "And hopefully, she'll have found my note by then."

"And hopefully, you'll stop being a self-sabotaging dummy," Garrett teased, raising his now half-empty wine bottle in a mock toast. "To new beginnings… or at least, to not messing up too badly."

Alex shook his head, laughing softly. "I'll drink to that." And as he took another sip of wine, he silently promised himself he wouldn't let fear deny him a second chance at something real—especially if that something involved Maia Collins.

CHAPTER FOURTEEN

*A*nother morning, Maia thought as she tied the laces of her sneakers. She paused, staring at the faint reflection of herself in the hallway mirror. She looked tired—maybe not physically, but there was a weariness in her eyes that spoke of more than just missed sleep.

She'd chugged a mug of hot tea the moment she rolled out of bed, hoping the warmth would soothe the knots in her stomach. In the past, these knots came from fear of jogging alone, but now they twisted for a different reason—because she half expected *not* to be alone.

A soft sigh escaped her lips as she straightened. Her hand rested on the golden knob of her front door, but she hesitated, glancing over her shoulder at the house's still interior. An odd combination of longing and resolution fluttered through her.

Jogging by herself for two days in a row had been easier than she'd thought. She'd expected a panic attack to seize her partway through, but somehow she'd pushed on, one foot after another, lost in the swirl of her own thoughts. *If only the reason for her success didn't hurt so much—Alex's absence had occupied her mind enough to distract her from those old fears.*

Swallowing back the ache in her chest, Maia took a deep breath, willing herself not to cling to any false hope. *He hasn't shown for two days. Face it, Maia: he might not come back.* She closed her eyes briefly, recalling Derek's phone call, the rush of fear, and then the sting of missing Alex's comfort. *Relying on others is a weakness,* she silently reminded herself. *And you, of all people, should know better.*

She opened the door, ready to face another run alone, but froze in shock.

There, standing in the light of the early morning, was none other than Alex—dressed in a sleek black tracksuit, his hair ruffled by the breeze. Her mouth went dry, and her heart thumped in her ears. *What is he doing here?*

"Alex?" she managed, closing the door behind her as he stepped forward.

"Maia," he greeted, his tone quiet but urgent. "Did you see my note?"

His voice, a little breathless, caught her off guard. She could only stare for a beat. *A note?* Her mind spun, grappling with the question.

"My note," Alex repeated, stopping just in front of her welcome mat. "I left it there for you." His expression hovered between hopeful and apologetic. "I would have called, but... um... I didn't ask for your number."

His words tumbled out, and Maia felt a complicated mix of relief and frustration spark inside her. *So he did try to contact me.* She inhaled, trying to steady the flutter in her stomach.

"Wait, a note?" she asked, forcing a calm tone into her voice, though her pulse hammered in her throat.

A gust of wind blew, pulling at Alex's hair. He seemed almost sheepish as he gestured to the mat. "Yes, under the mat. Did you see it?" He tried to keep his voice steady, but an edge of desperation clung to each syllable, as though he feared her response.

Maia's anger, which had been simmering for two days, began

to ebb. *He left a note—maybe this was all just a misunderstanding.* She cleared her throat, hugging her arms around her chest. "I didn't see any note," she confessed, glancing down at her porch. She stepped aside, watching as Alex knelt to lift the mat. "It's been windy these past few days. Maybe it blew away?"

Her mind reeled with the memory of how, just yesterday, she'd come home to find a flyer from the local diner pinned against her porch railing by a rock. *Could the wind have scattered Alex's note, too?*

"Must have," Alex groaned, standing upright with a weary sigh. "So, you just thought I chose not to show up for two days without explaining, huh?"

It was the sincerity in his eyes that unraveled her the most. She felt her chest tighten, torn between lingering anger and a rush of fondness. "What? No, no, I…" She swallowed hard, feeling the heat creep up her neck. "It wasn't a problem at all. I didn't even give it much thought, actually."

She lied, or tried to, but her voice wavered. *We both know I'm lying,* she admitted inwardly.

"Oh," Alex said, the corners of his mouth drooping slightly. "Oh…" His tone mirrored disappointment. "Why would you?"

That small flicker in his eyes, of regret and maybe hurt, tugged at her heart. Maia felt her cheeks warm further. Suddenly, the truth tumbled out, pushing aside her pride.

"I'm kidding," she said, voice trembling at the edges. "You had me wondering about you all day for both days you were gone." She folded her arms, trying to appear collected. "So, you left a note?"

"Yes." Alex raked a hand through his hair and exhaled a short laugh that was more self-conscious than amused. "I'm really stupid for not thinking to slip it under your door—and even stupider for not asking for your number when we first decided to jog together."

A little prickle of relief coursed through her. *So we're on the same page about that.* She found herself smirking despite everything. "You wanted to ask for my number from the start?"

"I'm saying that I *should* have," Alex corrected, though a shy smile touched his lips. "Then I could've sent a text about my business meeting—or even stayed in touch while I was gone."

Maia's heart pounded at the unexpected tenderness in his voice. She fought the urge to giggle, a swirl of excitement and nerves coursing through her. "You… would have wanted to stay in touch?" she asked quietly, stepping forward to the sidewalk.

He followed, matching her pace. "Yes," he replied simply. "If not for anything else, then to check how you were doing. I know running alone was never your favorite thing after what happened."

She inhaled, letting the fresh morning air fill her lungs. *It's sweet that he would care about my anxieties.* "That would've been thoughtful," she confessed, a tiny smile curving her lips. Though she tried not to show it, a bloom of warmth spread in her chest at his admission.

They stepped into the street's calm hush, side by side. A few early-rising neighbors opened their doors, fetching newspapers from the lawn or turning on porch lights. Maia barely noticed them—her focus was pinned on the man next to her.

"I would've wanted to know how you were doing in general, too," Alex added, voice soft. "Would it have been okay if I'd checked in?"

Her steps faltered for half a second. She turned to face him, letting the question echo in her head. *Would it have been okay?* She felt her heart skip. "That would've been nice," she said, glancing down to hide her grin.

Alex let out a short, relieved chuckle. Maia caught his eyes flick to her face, observing her reaction.

Something in the moment felt freeing, as though the tension that had weighed her down dissolved. *We're just two people who messed up not exchanging numbers,* she thought. *We can fix that.*

Without overthinking, she stopped and held out her hand. "Give me your phone. I'll put my number in for you."

Alex froze for an instant, the corners of his mouth quirking up. "Here you go," he said, pulling his phone from his pocket.

She punched in the digits, her pulse quickening as she labeled herself 'Maia.' Once Alex texted her, she saved his number as 'Alex J.' on her own screen. "Problem solved," she said, her voice dancing with a hint of satisfaction.

"Problem solving is pretty darn cool," Alex quipped, returning the phone to his pocket.

"Shall we?" Maia gestured to the sidewalk, the corners of her eyes crinkling in a contained smile.

"Lead the way," Alex replied, returning her expression with one of his own, a softness in his usually guarded gaze.

They set off at a steady jog, the morning air still crisp enough to nip at Maia's cheeks. She felt an unexpected giddiness in her stride, a pleasant awareness of Alex matching her pace. Their breathing found a natural rhythm, quiet but in sync.

"So, business trip?" Maia prompted, remembering the reason he'd vanished.

"Yeah, to Atlanta," Alex replied. "Had a client who insisted on meeting me face-to-face for some design changes. Happens occasionally."

"Do you go to Atlanta often?" she asked, curiosity burning in her chest.

Alex nodded. "Often enough. It's the closest big city. The occasional on-site job is part of freelance life, I guess."

Maia arched a brow, picking up the pace slightly. "Must be intense, catering to demanding clients."

He chuckled, as if imagining a specific situation. "It can be. But it's *mostly* manageable."

She detected a subtle tension as his tone faltered for a second. *He's remembering the divorce.* She decided to tread gently.

"Especially since your divorce?" she ventured, voice soft.

A flicker of surprise crossed his features. "Yeah, actually," he admitted. "Work used to feel like a break from my personal life, but once your personal life implodes, it has a way of bleeding into everything."

Maia swallowed, nodding in empathy. "I feel like a totally different person after mine, so I understand. Sometimes it's like I can't go back to who I was before."

Alex offered a quiet hum of agreement. "Same. It's like I spent so long trying to force myself into a shape that didn't fit. Once the marriage ended, I realized I needed a completely different outlook."

The conversation fell away, leaving the gentle *thump-thump* of their shoes on the pavement. A sliver of sun peeked over the rooftops, warming Maia's shoulders. *This is so easy,* she thought. The quiet understanding between them felt comforting, like they were forging a connection over shared pain.

After a while, they slowed to a walk, letting the energy of Sweetgum stir around them. A group of older women in matching turquoise tracksuits marched past on the opposite side, nearly bowling over a pair of young girls holding backpacks.

"Wow, did you see that?" Maia exclaimed, eyes widening. "They almost knocked those girls down!"

Alex smirked. "That's the hit-and-run crew. They've been speed-walking around here for years. It's kind of their unofficial trademark—nobody stands a chance if they cross paths."

Maia huffed, half amused, half scandalized. "Seems a bit rude. They might need a lesson in courtesy."

Alex laughed under his breath, and they resumed a gentle jog that soon morphed into a stroll as the streets grew busier. They chatted seamlessly—about random cities they hadn't visited, about how Alex had never traveled beyond a handful of states. Maia found herself diving into memories of her last branch job in Savannah, describing the chaotic conventions she'd attended. Alex listened intently, eyes bright with interest.

Finally, Alex slowed in front of an alley leading to a more commercial section of town. Maia recognized a few of the local shops opening their shutters for the day.

"… so, losing your aunt and moving here all at once must've been a big shift," Alex said gently.

Maia nodded, rubbing her palms together. The day was warming up, yet her hands felt clammy. "Yeah, it was. But it also gave me purpose, you know? I needed something positive to focus on."

He offered her a small, encouraging smile. "Speaking of the house, are we still on for cleanup later?"

Something inside her tensed. She scuffed the toe of her sneaker against the sidewalk. "Oh, actually, there's not much left to do. While you were gone, I pretty much finished everything up." She shrugged, remembering how she'd poured her anxieties into polishing floors and wiping windows. "So, yeah… no need for you to come over again. The house is practically spotless."

"You managed all that in just two days?" Alex asked, sounding both impressed and disappointed.

She forced a casual shrug. "Well, it was mostly minor stuff—dusting, polishing. You did the heavy lifting before you left."

He crossed his arms, cocking an eyebrow. "You never cease to amaze me."

A delicate warmth bloomed in her chest at his compliment. She opened her mouth to respond but stopped when Alex spoke first.

"So, when can I see the finished product?" he asked, a playful spark in his eye. "I never got the full house tour, you know."

Maia fiddled with her phone in her pocket. The invitation hovered on her tongue, and her heart thumped with a sudden flurry of nerves. "Right, I guess you haven't…" She chewed her lip. *Why am I so hesitant? We're just friends. Right?* "You can stop by if you want."

As if on cue, a passerby shuffled by them, forcing them to step aside. Alex gently guided Maia out of the way, his hands briefly on her shoulders. Even after he let go, the impression of warmth lingered.

"Unless you're still busy," she added, half-hoping he'd say no so she didn't have to wade into confusing feelings, half-hoping he'd say yes.

"I'd love to," Alex answered immediately. "Would six be okay?"

Her heart soared. She tried not to let it show on her face but couldn't keep a small smile from forming. "Yes, six works."

They stood there, sharing a charged silence, until suddenly a voice called out from a building just behind them.

"Hey, you!"

Maia jolted, turning to see a policeman standing outside the local station, his uniform unmistakable. She recognized him from the day she'd first reported the robbery.

"You're the lady who reported an attempted robbery, right?" the officer asked, stepping closer. "Got a moment? We've got some updates."

It took Maia a heartbeat to realize they'd drifted so close to the station. She glanced at Alex, whose brows lifted in mild surprise. *Well, so much for a relaxing end to our morning.*

"Sure," she said, swallowing down the flicker of nerves.

Inside, the station felt quieter than usual. Only two policemen seemed to be on duty. One leaned against a wall, sipping coffee from a thermos, while the other—the one who'd called them—sat behind the desk, rummaging through a folder. Maia and Alex hovered near the waiting area, the wooden chairs looking as unwelcoming as always.

"All right, so last night our investigators managed to find someone who matched your description," the officer at the desk began. "Kid from Peachwood, known to have family problems. He's apparently got a record of petty theft, and the timeline fits with when you were robbed."

Maia's gaze darted to Alex. She felt a mix of relief and apprehension swirl in her stomach. *A kid?*

"He was reported missing from his home around the same time as your robbery and just returned two days ago," the officer continued. "We told him to come in for questioning this morning—figured you could ID him."

"So, it's a teenager?" Maia asked, her voice laced with disbelief. Part of her had pictured a hardened criminal or a grown thug. *This changes everything... or does it?*

Alex's arms folded tight over his chest, the tension in his jaw flickering. "Even if he's a kid, that doesn't erase the harm he did," he said quietly. "But it explains a lot."

"He's still at fault," the officer agreed, leaning back in his chair. "Anyway, do you want to press charges once we confirm he's our guy? Juvie might be the only deterrent if he's that far gone."

"That feels... harsh," Maia said softly, sharing a look with Alex.

Alex nodded, an edge of compassion in his expression. "Yeah. No one's condoning what he did, but it's easy for a kid to spiral if we punish him without giving him a real chance to change."

The officer grunted. "Up to you. But it's better to decide once you see him, I guess."

He motioned to them to wait, and before Maia could protest, three people entered the lobby from another hallway. Two uniformed officers and a tall, lanky boy with his head lowered. One of the cops nudged him forward.

"Here he is. Brought him in first thing like we said."

The teen wore a matching hoodie and sweatpants, a cap

pulled low over his eyes. Maia's blood chilled. She recognized the silhouette. *The same posture, the same quiet hostility.*

"Oh my God," she whispered, tension rippling through her limbs as she rose from her seat. Alex stood too, his stance protective but calm.

One of the officers nudged the boy. "Go on, Brian. Let them see you clearly. No point in hiding your face now."

Reluctantly, the teen lifted his chin, eyes meeting Maia's. For a moment, she saw a flash of anger—fueled by shame, perhaps? He had the same brazen aura, but now it felt subdued, weighted by the presence of authority figures.

"He says he can't remember this specific robbery," the other cop drawled, "but he admits he's stolen so many phones and wallets he's lost track. Sound about right?"

"This is definitely the guy," Alex said, stepping closer. His tone held a quiet gravity, and Maia's heart squeezed. She knew he was thinking back to the moment he'd wrestled the phone away.

Alex's gaze locked on Brian. "I hope you realize how wrong this was," he said softly, but firmly. "Stealing from people isn't just about the stuff—it's about violating their sense of safety. There are better ways to handle whatever you're dealing with."

Brian's jaw clenched, a rebellious glint in his eye. He glanced away, refusing to respond. Maia studied him, feeling an odd pang of pity. *He's just a kid.*

"So, pressing charges, or what?" another officer cut in, looking bored. "Community service might be an option if it's a first-time offense in our jurisdiction, but it's your call."

Maia parted her lips, trying to steady her breathing. *Community service felt more humane.* She glanced at Alex, who gave her an encouraging nod, letting her decide.

"No," she said, shaking her head. "I don't want to press charges. Community service sounds more appropriate."

The policeman shrugged, scribbling a note in his folder. "All right, that's that, then."

Brian's posture sagged, relief flickering across his features, though he still wouldn't meet Maia's eyes.

"Hey," Alex interjected, catching the teen's attention for one last moment. "When I was your age, I had my share of anger and confusion. Don't let yourself get stuck there. There are better outlets." His voice softened, sincerity lacing each word.

Brian offered nothing more than a sullen nod. The officers led him away, leaving the waiting room empty and echoing with tension.

"Heavy metal's pretty effective," Alex muttered, turning to Maia with a faint grin.

She lifted an eyebrow, a ghost of a laugh escaping her lips. "Heavy metal?"

He gave a small shrug, the corners of his mouth lifting. "Kept me sane back then. Sort of. Long story."

"I'd love to hear it one day," Maia teased gently, a sense of relief settling over her as they headed back out into the cool air.

Once on the sidewalk, she breathed in deeply, shaking off the residual tension of that confrontation. "So... cleaning?" she asked, her voice lighter now that the weight of the situation had eased.

"Cleaning it is," Alex agreed. A subtle warmth shone in his dark eyes as he walked beside her.

They continued down the street, side by side. And though the day had begun with confusion and tension, Maia felt a surge of calm settle in her chest, comforted by the knowledge that they'd face whatever came next—together.

Maia's body still hadn't recovered from all the back-breaking work she'd put into cleaning. She could feel the slight ache in her shoulders and lower back as she guided Alex into Aunt Dianne's living room.

"It's probably hard to notice, but the floors are way shinier than they were before," she said, gesturing toward the gleaming boards. "Do you see how your reflection is in the floorboards?" She spun in a half-circle, flicking on the overhead light. The warm glow revealed a space that looked renewed, almost like a different house from the one Alex had first seen. "It's like a brand-new house, don't you think?"

Alex walked in slowly, hands in his pockets. He'd sent her a text around five-thirty to confirm the time, but Maia had been looking forward to seeing him again all day, her nerves flickering with the possibility that perhaps their jogging partnership —*or whatever it was*—might soon end. The thought had clung to her, making every hour at work crawl.

"I'll admit that the air is a lot less stuffy," he said, inhaling deeply as he neared the couch. "There's also an amazing smell that wasn't here before." He closed his eyes, taking in the aroma. "Is that lavender?"

"Yes, it is," Maia replied, her voice tinged with pride. She nodded at a small air freshener plugged into the wall near an armchair. "I plugged that in before I left yesterday. Aunt Dianne really liked floral scents, so this felt right."

She noticed Alex's gaze flick around the living room, taking in the spotless surfaces, the polished tables, the curtains drawn neatly aside. She could see his expression soften in quiet appreciation.

"I'm guessing that's why she enjoyed gardening so much," Alex said, shifting his attention to the stairs. "You finished upstairs too?"

Maia folded her hands anxiously. "Um… yes, actually. Like I said, everything is good as new." She bit her lip, recalling how she'd poured her lingering grief into sweeping, dusting, and polishing until her arms burned.

"Oh, great," he said, crossing the living room toward the staircase. Then he paused, casting her a questioning look. "May I?"

The sudden wave of anxiety that washed over Maia caught her off guard. *Why do I feel so uneasy about him seeing Aunt Dianne's bedroom?* "Um…" she started, searching her own feelings. She wanted to share, but a knot tightened in her chest.

"Everything okay?" Alex's voice held gentle concern.

"Yes. And yes, let's go. I'll show you her room, the guest room, and the bathroom." Maia forced a small smile and started up the stairs, taking a deep breath to steady the flutter in her stomach. *It's fine,* she reminded herself. *I'm okay.*

They walked along a thin printed mat that ran the length of the corridor. Both their shoes clicked against the wood beneath it, echoing in the quiet. *He's so close,* she thought, hyper-aware of his presence just behind her. The faint warmth of him at her back made her pulse thrum at an oddly comforting pace.

At the first door, Maia flicked on the light switch. "Ta-da," she announced, stepping in with a faint hum. Alex followed, his footsteps slow as he took in the changes.

"You don't have a 'before' picture of this room to understand how much better it looks," she said, placing a hand on the edge of a dresser. "But just know that I did a good job." The row of perfume bottles shimmered under the overhead light, each one carefully placed. The bed had been made with fresh linens and a new comforter, while pastel curtains replaced the old, faded ones. A daisy-scented air freshener glowed softly in the corner.

"Very nice," Alex murmured, crossing to the bed. He spun around, surveying every corner. "Cozy. This whole house has a certain warmth to it." He exhaled, turning back to Maia. "Reminds me of home."

Her stomach flipped at the compliment. "Your mom and dad had a pretty good place for you, right?" she asked, tucking a strand of hair behind her ear. The memory of Mrs. Zhang's bustling warmth at the restaurant sprang to mind, a testament to the environment Alex must have grown up in.

"They sure did," he said, smiling in that subdued way that made Maia's chest tighten. She followed his gaze as it drifted to the still-made bed, and for a fleeting second, an odd sadness passed through her. *Aunt Dianne will never see this again.*

"Yeah," Maia whispered, blinking to clear the sudden sting in her eyes. "Okay, now for the bathroom and guest room."

She led him down the hallway, showing off the newly scrubbed tiles and meticulously cleaned surfaces. Alex commented with genuine admiration, and Maia offered playful bows in return. *It's nice,* she thought, *having someone other than Aimee or me to appreciate this effort.* The reminder of the last few months of loneliness clung to her, but Alex's presence lightened it like a gentle breeze.

They headed back downstairs, Maia feeling both accomplished and oddly vulnerable.

"Wait, what about that room down there?" Alex asked, pointing beyond the guest room door.

Maia's smile tightened. A locked door stood at the far end of the corridor, out of the way. "That's just the room I used to stay in when I visited. I cleaned it up too, but... not as well as the others." She forced a laugh, though a prickle of nerves tightened her chest. *Why am I hesitant?*

Alex kept his gaze on her. "I don't want to make you uncomfortable."

She blinked, trying to steady herself. *He doesn't know what he's saying. It's just an old room.* "No, it's okay. You can take a look," she insisted, heading to the last door despite the uneasy flutter in her stomach. *You're not that fragile, Maia.*

The air hit her the moment she opened the door—a stale, musty scent. She flicked on a switch, the overhead light revealing a small space with a single bed and a window draped in thin curtains. A tinge of storage odor lingered, and Maia prayed Alex wouldn't notice how her shoulders tensed.

"Here it is." She swallowed, forcing a casual tone. The memories of her teenage years haunted every inch of the space. She saw herself at sixteen, curled up against Aunt Dianne, sobbing over her latest heartbreak. *Stop it,* she scolded herself.

Alex scanned the room quietly, from the dusty bookshelf near the door to the faded carpet by the bed. "It feels lived-in," he remarked, stepping farther inside. "Like someone's still here. But..." He trailed off, running a finger across a shelf. A thick line of dust collected on his skin. His brow furrowed as he glanced at Maia.

She said nothing, hugging her arms as a thousand memories stormed her mind—Aunt Dianne's warm hugs, the nights spent crying over heartbreak, the lullabies that used to drift from the speaker on the bedside table. *It's just a space now... no Aunt Dianne, no comforting smell of her cooking drifting upstairs.*

A tender warmth touched her shoulder, and she looked up to see Alex, concern etched in the set of his jaw. "We can leave if you want," he offered softly. "You don't have to force this."

She let out a shaky breath, tears burning the back of her eyes. "This is so stupid," she muttered, moving to the bed and sitting down heavily. The mattress squeaked, echoing the frailty in her heart. "Ugh, what is wrong with me?" She propped her elbows on her knees, pressing her palms against her temples.

Alex joined her, the mattress dipping under his weight. She sensed him close, and the comfort that emanated from him nearly broke her defenses. She took in his scent—a mix of clean fabric and a lingering trace of his aftershave.

"I'm sorry," she whispered, a tear slipping free. "This is so embarrassing. I don't know why I didn't just lie and say I never got around to cleaning this room. It's not a big deal." Her shoulders trembled. "It's just hard, you know? Even though it's been months..."

"There's no textbook for how long grief should last," Alex murmured. "Everyone's journey is different."

She sniffed, tears making her vision blur. "I thought making the house perfect would fix something inside me. Aunt Dianne always loved keeping things tidy, so I figured if I cleaned it well, I'd get closure." She laughed bitterly, scrubbing her eyes with the heel of her hand. "But she's gone. She's not going to see any of this. It'll just get messy again sooner or later."

She lifted her head, gazing at the slanted portion of the ceiling above the bed—remembering how she and Aunt Dianne once plastered glow-in-the-dark stars there. "I don't know what to do. I can't live here alone—it's too big and too full of ghosts." She rubbed the ring at her necklace, the cold metal centering her. "But I hate the thought of selling it. It feels… wrong."

The silence wrapped around them like a shroud. She caught Alex's eyes flicking to her necklace, sympathy reflected in his expression.

"This wasn't supposed to go like this," Maia muttered, voice cracking.

Alex breathed out slowly, placing a reassuring hand on her shoulder again. "You don't have to figure it all out right now," he said, his tone gentle but firm. "Sometimes forcing closure only makes it harder. It's okay to be… in-between." His palm lingered a moment longer, steady against her trembling frame. "I guess I sound like a broken record, but people heal at their own pace."

A weak laugh escaped her lips. "Does that make me stubborn?"

He shook his head, the corner of his mouth lifting. "Just means you're human. Trust me, I get it. I'm the same."

She drew in a trembling breath, lifting her eyes to meet his. "Is that why you told that boy to try music as an outlet?" she asked, recalling the oddly intimate moment at the station.

Alex smiled crookedly. "My teenage self had rage issues, so

yeah—loud music and I were close friends." His eyes flicked downward. "But even that didn't fully solve anything. It just bought me time until I could grow up."

"I see." Maia sniffled, forcing a shaky smile. "All feelings are valid, right?"

"Exactly." He held her gaze a second longer than expected, and she felt the warmth radiating between them. A flicker of something heavier, more profound, hummed in the space.

Gently, Alex shifted, standing from the bed. "I truly think your aunt would be proud of all you've done. Sometimes doing it for ourselves is enough, but it's nice to think she's smiling wherever she is." He exhaled. "Did that help at all? Or am I just spouting clichés?"

Maia angled her head upward, watching him fill the small space. "I don't know," she admitted softly. She found it impossible to lie to him anymore. "But thank you."

"That's okay," Alex said, offering her a faint smile. "It's getting late, and you said you have work tomorrow, right?"

Maia jolted, checking the time on her phone. "You're right. Thanks for the reminder." She stood abruptly, the blood rushing from her head, momentarily dizzy from the emotional upheaval.

They moved side by side out of the room, drifting down the hallway in a silence that spoke volumes. *This closeness... it feels more precious than anything I've known in a while*, Maia thought, hugging her arms tighter around herself.

Once downstairs, Maia locked up, the crisp night air making her shiver. A subtle pang twisted her chest as she realized that, with the robber caught, Alex might not have a reason to be around anymore. *We're out of excuses*, she realized, sliding the key from the lock with a heavy sigh.

"All good?" Alex asked, a questioning tilt to his head.

She forced a small nod. "Yes. Thank you. For everything. For keeping me safe, helping me around the house, talking to that kid…" She trailed off, chewing the inside of her cheek. "You've been incredibly kind."

Alex smiled gently, his hands slipping into his jacket pockets. "It was my pleasure." A pause hung in the cold air. "So, I'll see you around?"

The familiar ache blossomed in Maia's chest. "Yes," she whispered, *please say we'll see each other again.* "Tomorrow for our run, and then…"

His expression shifted, a soft spark lighting behind his dark eyes. "Actually, maybe we could grab lunch after? If you're up for it."

Her pulse jolted. *Was that an invitation, or just a friend offer?* She swallowed the sudden tangle of nerves. "Lunch? Yes. That'd be great." She couldn't hide the swell of excitement warming her body.

"Where should we meet?" Alex asked. *He almost sounded shy,* she noticed, which made the moment even more endearing.

Maia fiddled with the edge of her sleeve. "My best friend and I usually eat at Rochelle's Diner on Main Street. She's… a local legend, apparently." She laughed lightly. "We could go there, if you like. I'd enjoy showing you my favorite spot."

"Rochelle's? My mom's best friend owns it." Alex nodded, the corner of his mouth quirking up. "I've eaten her cooking more times than I can count."

"Great!" Maia said, a little too eagerly, feeling her cheeks heat. "So, tomorrow at lunch."

"Yes," Alex echoed, the soft half-smile lingering as if it, too, was reluctant to leave. "But we'll still do our usual run in the morning, so it won't be too long until we meet again."

Her heart fluttered at the thought. "Then it's settled," she murmured, smiling back.

"It's definitely settled," Alex said with a gentle assurance.

And as the night wrapped around them, Maia felt her worries slip into the background—replaced by the quiet hope that this new connection might be every bit as warm and meaningful as it felt in that moment.

CHAPTER FIFTEEN

*E*verything—from her playful giggles to the way her eyes lit up when he'd asked her to lunch—revealed Maia's anticipation. Alex couldn't pretend he was any less excited; he'd spent a good chunk of last night imagining all sorts of scenarios for their date. Even calling it a date in his own head felt like standing at the edge of a cliff—both exhilarating and terrifying.

He leaned back on the couch, laptop balanced on his thighs, and clicked "send" on an email containing one of the finished marketing campaigns for a client. Odie lay sprawled at the foot of the sofa, occasionally thumping his tail against the floor. With a groan, Alex ran his hands over his face. *Am I really doing this?*

That morning's jog had gone like any other, except for the subtle, electric charge that seemed to hover between him and Maia. They couldn't resist smiling at each other—like a pair of teenagers rediscovering the thrill of a crush. Alex had tried to keep himself composed, but the plan evaporated the moment Maia greeted him with that bright smile at sunrise. *Is this the* right call? he wondered. Did he dare open himself up again after the blow Phoebe dealt him?

The day outside was unusually clear. Sunlight streamed in through the kitchen windows, throwing bright, golden rectangles across the counters. After his shower, Alex paused to listen to the chirping of birds—a simple detail he might've ignored in his old life but now found comforting. He opened another project file on his laptop, typing away. When I asked Maia out, I decided this is a date. That thought both thrilled and scared him.

If it is a date, I'll have to expose my heart again, he reminded himself. But maybe he'd be more guarded this time around. For now, though, he'd let the day unfold and hope it led to something good. Deep down, he yearned for it. There was something about Maia that made him want to believe love could be worth the risk.

"How long have your mom and Rochelle known each other?" Maia asked, leaning forward with curiosity.

Seeing her in anything but sweats or workout gear was new to Alex, and he found himself appreciating the sight. She wore a fitted black jacket over matching trousers, and a deep-blue blouse peeked beneath. A gentle, floral perfume surrounded her. Everything about her outfit radiated a quiet confidence that struck him. It was very Maia—somehow simple, comfortable, and lovely.

Alex took a sip of water, glancing around at the lively diner. The lunchtime rush was in full swing; waitresses glided past with trays of steaming plates, and customers chatted loudly at nearly every table. "Probably most of their lives. I think they first met when my parents opened their restaurant. That was... I guess they were in their twenties. Now they're old."

He said this last part with a teasing grin that made Maia giggle. "They may be old in age, but their hearts seem young. I've never actually talked to Rochelle or your mom, but from a distance, they seem pretty energetic."

She rubbed her palms together, revealing a hint of nervousness that she was clearly trying to hide. Alex felt a pang of his own nerves—why am I fidgeting, too?

"You're observant," he said, offering a gentle smile. "My mom can be a tad... over-energetic in person. Some days, I think it's too much. But she's been that way forever." He put down his water glass and settled into his seat. "How was your day, Maia?"

She lowered her gaze as she shrugged. "Busy. Really busy. But I'm just relieved I haven't been forced to take leave like my boss wanted a few days ago."

Alex blinked, leaning in. "Your boss wanted you to take leave? Why would she do that? Something happen?"

A waitress slowed by their table, but they both shook their heads and motioned they were fine, so she bustled off again. The diner smelled like a blend of fresh coffee, bacon grease, and pie crust—comforting and homey, though a bit overwhelming.

Maia stiffened slightly. "It's nothing major. I was just a bit off for a while, but I'm better now. My boss got worried. She's..." She paused as though searching for the right words. "She's very into mental health awareness. If she thinks I'm overworked or unfocused, she'll practically force me to rest."

Alex frowned. Something in her voice hinted at a deeper story, but he decided not to press. "All right... If you're okay, then good."

Before Maia could reply, a waitress arrived with their orders —an aromatic turkey sandwich for Maia and a plate of fried chicken and fries for Alex. They exchanged polite thanks, and the woman vanished again into the bustling sea of customers.

Alex watched Maia take her first bite. "Anyway," he continued, cutting into his chicken, "my day was decent. I mostly stayed in pajamas, napped between assignments... you know, living the freelance dream."

She scrunched her nose in mock envy. "Must be nice."

"I don't mean to brag, but it is," he teased, appreciating how her eyes sparked with interest at every word. "And since you asked, yeah, it's just me, my work, and the silence of home. Sometimes I'll play with Odie if I need a break."

Maia paused mid-chew. "You have a dog?"

He couldn't hide the amusement in his voice. "So you are an animal lover?"

She swallowed, setting her sandwich down. "Well, I wouldn't say I'm a huge animal lover, but I don't mind them. I just never had one myself, so it's a bit foreign to me. But now I'm curious—what's Odie like?"

"Sweetest mutt you'll ever meet. My ex originally wanted a dog, but after the divorce, I ended up keeping him." Alex felt a tug of pain recalling the messy logistics of splitting everything after the marriage ended. "It's funny how he's the best thing I got out of that entire relationship."

Maia brushed her hair behind her ear. "Wow. So do you think we'll ever get to meet? Or, I mean, me and Odie?" She laughed shyly at her own question.

Alex found himself oddly pleased by her interest. "I'd be happy to introduce you if you want," he said, trying to gauge her reaction. She seemed genuinely excited by the idea.

"Sure! Just so long as he's not a biter or anything," she joked.

Alex let out a low chuckle. "No, he's a sweetheart. You'll see." He popped a fry into his mouth and sat back. "So, you keep making it sound like listening to music while working is some elusive dream. Isn't it allowed at your workplace?"

She rolled her eyes playfully. "It's not that it's banned. I just imagine you at home cranking the volume to max, rocking out as loud as you want without coworkers bursting in."

"Ah." Alex lifted his brows. "You got that assumption from me recommending heavy metal to that kid, right?"

She cocked her head, swirling the straw in her drink. "Exactly. If you're not a metalhead, why did you suggest that particular genre to him? I'd have guessed you were more into calmer stuff."

Alex shrugged, feeling a hint of nostalgia. "I listened to it a lot as a teenager, especially when I was dealing with anger or stress. Something about those pounding drums and raw vocals helped me let it all out. But that doesn't mean it's my main go-to now."

Maia's eyes widened a fraction. "You, a teenager full of rage? I can't picture it."

He snorted. "Trust me, I had my moments."

The surprise on her face made him laugh inside. The look quickly gave way to curiosity. "So what do you listen to these days?"

"Everything, honestly. I'm not big on just one style—jazz, pop, RnB, reggae... I'll sample them all." He considered her thoughtfully. "What about you? Any favorites?"

She brightened. "I love abstract lyrics—stuff that makes me think twice about what I'm hearing. Especially when I was younger, if I felt misunderstood, I'd find comfort in those kinds of songs. Now, I'm open to pretty much everything, but the more meaningful or unique the lyrics, the more I like it."

He nodded, recalling a memory. "Reminds me of a show I caught in Atlanta once. The artist had this line about love— something about it stealing a piece of them every time they touched it, but they still willingly reached out. It was so dramatic and kind of sad, yet it stuck with me."

"Do you believe that?" she asked, arching a brow.

He paused, the words echoing in his mind—steals a piece of me every time... "No," he said eventually. "I understand the fear behind it, though."

She studied him for a moment, then gave a nod of approval. "I don't believe it either. Love might hurt sometimes, but it shouldn't be like that lyric all the time."

They shared a fleeting laugh that felt oddly intimate, like an inside joke. The conversation settled into a peaceful lull as they continued eating, the diner's clamor forming a comforting backdrop.

At one point, Alex noticed a waitress at the counter staring openly at them, a grin on her face. When he turned, she quickly spun around, pretending to busy herself with a stack of menus.

"Who's that?" he asked, nodding subtly toward the counter.

Maia followed his gaze and smiled. "Oh, that's Aimee—my best friend. She's the one I usually have lunch with here." Her eyes sparkled mischievously. "I'm sure she's itching to come over and eavesdrop. You'd like her, though. Maybe I can introduce you two properly sometime."

He nodded, curious about the friend Maia mentioned so often. He was about to respond when Maia's phone vibrated on the table. She glanced at it and let out a tiny gasp. "I'm late," she mumbled, eyes widening in alarm.

Alex quickly wiped his mouth, dropping the napkin on his empty plate. "I'm sorry. Did I talk too much?" He felt a small stab of guilt; he hadn't realized so much time had passed.

"No!" she insisted, scrambling to gather her things. "I enjoyed every word. Really." She rose, brushing crumbs from her jacket. "We should do this again—like, regularly."

"I'd like that," he said softly. It warmed him to hear she wanted more time with him.

She slipped off to the restroom, returning after a minute with her hair smoothed and a faint dab of fresh lipstick. "Thank you again," she said as they left the diner, the midday sun hitting them. "You didn't have to pay for both of us."

He waved it off. "I wanted to." He couldn't meet her eyes for a moment, battling the swirl of contentment and self-consciousness.

They walked to the sidewalk, and he watched Maia's graceful movements as she checked the direction of traffic. It felt surreal—just days ago, they were near-strangers passing each other on a jogging route. Now, seeing her in her classy work attire, feeling the closeness between them, stirred a flutter in his chest.

Eventually, she turned to him, her eyes searching his. "I need to head back to the office," she said regretfully. "I'll see you tomorrow, though?"

He nodded, forcing a lightness into his tone. "Absolutely. I can't wait."

With a lingering smile, Maia waved and strode away, slipping into the throng of passersby. Alex stood rooted, his gaze following her until she disappeared around the corner. Her perfume still hung in the air, and he swore he could feel her presence even after she'd gone.

She's all I can see, he thought. *She's all I can feel.*

"Wow," he muttered, raking a hand through his hair. So much for maintaining distance. Instead, he'd plunged headlong into the possibility of something new, something hopeful.

He tried to recall the last time he'd felt this kind of buoyancy after spending time with someone. With Phoebe, it had been an intense, whirlwind romance—but beneath the rush, there'd always been an unease he could never place. This felt different. Warmer, steadier. Like they were on the same page without constantly second-guessing each other's motives.

At this point, it would be criminal to leave things as they are, he told himself. I want to see what this could turn into. For the first time in a long time, Alex felt excited about the future. He wasn't about to let that feeling slip away.

Maia was the highlight of his day... and he couldn't wait to see what else she might highlight in his life.

CHAPTER SIXTEEN

Dinner was lasagna and red wine tonight, courtesy of Aimee's last-minute grocery run after a chaotic shift at the diner. She'd shared all the day's drama—like the customer who changed their order at least three times in a row—but apparently, that wasn't what had really caught her attention. No, it was what she'd seen when Maia and Alex had met for lunch. And if her dramatic reenactment was any indication, Aimee had thoroughly enjoyed playing the role of an undercover matchmaker.

Maia sat at Aimee's kitchen table, fiddling with the stem of her wine glass. She hated how her heart pounded like a teenager's at the mere mention of Alex's name. He was just a man, right? A man who'd gone from good Samaritan to potential... something else. And a part of her wanted to bask in every replay of their lunch together.

"Stop. I was not looking at him like that," Maia complained, letting out a huff when Aimee launched into another over-the-top impression.

"Yes, you were." Aimee rapped the table next to her plate, face aglow with amusement. "He looked like he was mumbling in some mysterious low voice, and then you were all, 'Oh, Alex, you're so funny.'" She tipped her head to the side, adopting a dramatic swoon, before turning back with a sly grin. "Then you both laughed, and I swear the chemistry sizzled like bacon on a hot skillet."

Maia felt her cheeks flare. She stabbed a chunk of lasagna, swirling her fork around the melted cheese and minced meat before popping it into her mouth. "You're exaggerating. We were just talking."

"Right," Aimee drawled, barely hiding a smirk. "You keep telling yourself that. But you know perfectly well he asked you out to lunch for a reason. Especially after that emotional moment you two shared at Aunt Dianne's."

Maia's heart tightened at the memory—she'd nearly cried, and Alex had been so kind, so thoughtful. "We're just friends," she argued, though her own heart wasn't convinced. "That's all."

"Sure," Aimee teased, snapping her fingers with flair. "He's ready to go from bodyguard to boyfriend."

The mere thought made Maia's pulse jump. "Aimee, don't put ideas in my head. If you keep on, I'll start picturing myself in a white gown, walking down the aisle, and that's the last thing I need. It's not like I'm in a hurry to get serious with anyone."

Still, she couldn't deny how exciting the thought was. In the last few days, she'd found her imagination wandering, picturing Alex in different sweet, supportive scenarios. After all her heartbreak with Derek, part of her yearned for a safer kind of happiness. But could Alex really be that man?

She groaned inwardly. *What if I'm just making the same mistake all over again?*

Aimee paused, her forkful of lasagna hovering in midair. "What do you mean?"

Maia hesitated, fiddling with the ring on her necklace. Ever since Derek, that ring had remained a bittersweet reminder.

"I've worked too hard to piece myself back together. If I get involved with someone and it goes south… I can't relive that. I can't."

Aimee set down her fork, leaning in. "But you like him, right?"

Gazing at the ring's dull gleam, Maia sighed. "Yes, I do," she admitted softly. "But I also promised myself I wouldn't go down that road again."

"Why not?"

She gave a little shrug, fighting an urge to hide her face in her hands. "Didn't I just say? I'm terrified. Derek broke me in ways I never thought possible."

Aimee leaned back with a thoughtful expression. "You've been single for over a year, though. Your self-improvement journey was about learning to love yourself again— not swearing off relationships for the rest of time."

Maia looked away, suddenly uneasy. She tugged at the braids she'd recently taken out, now replaced by twists that dusted her shoulders. "I know, but Alex feels… too good. I don't want to trust someone too easily again."

An image of Alex at lunch popped into her mind: his quiet self-assurance, the way he'd listened with genuine interest. Part of her wanted to run headlong into the possibility of him, but another part recoiled at the risk.

Aimee sighed with exaggerated patience, scraping the last bit of sauce from her plate. "You already said he's been nothing but sweet—and from what I've seen with my own two eyes, there's no question the man is smitten. Are you really going to let one bad relationship stop you from giving this a chance?"

"I—" Maia paused, trying to formulate a response. "I guess I'm scared. Alex was so gentle last night when I got emotional, so… comforting. A big contrast from Derek's dismissive attitude in the end."

Aimee smacked her hands on the table. "The other guy could never," she declared triumphantly.

Maia huffed a laugh, her gaze lingering on the ring at her collarbone. "Derek was sweet once, too—then he stopped." A hollow ache pressed at her ribs. "I just can't do that all over again."

"Don't paint them with the same brush," Aimee insisted, carrying her dish to the sink. "You told me Derek gave off some pretty glaring red flags early on. Does Alex have any red flags?"

"No. He's been all green flags. Seriously," Maia conceded. "He hasn't done a single thing to make me doubt him. It's just… it's only been a few weeks. Am I naive to jump from zero to daydreaming about a future with him?"

Aimee snorted. "What can I say? Sometimes you click with someone right away. Doesn't mean you should overthink it. Plus, you're not exactly wearing your heart on your sleeve— you're being cautious, which is good. Just don't shut out all the good, too."

Maia grimaced, toying with the leftover lasagna on her plate. "Yeah, maybe…"

She rose to help Aimee clear the table, avoiding her friend's gaze. Inside, a swirl of anticipation and worry churned. *Yes, I like him, but is that enough to risk heartbreak again?*

LATER THAT NIGHT, after her usual skincare routine, Maia slipped into her comfy oversized sweater and settled in bed with a paperback novel. The soft glow of her bedside lamp illuminated the pages, highlighting the dramatic climax of the story. She'd promised herself she'd read more this year, and so far, it was going well—she found escape in the fictional worlds that, for once, didn't revolve around her anxieties.

Her phone rested nearby, the screen black. She glanced at it occasionally, half-hoping a message might pop up from Alex. *He did say goodnight earlier, so maybe not.* She turned a page, diving deeper into the fictional suspense.

Ring! Ring!

Maia nearly dropped her book. She sat up, her heart thumping. "It's eleven p.m. Who in their right mind…" Her voice trailed off when she saw the caller ID. Alex.

All the tension in her shoulders released in a rush. She pressed "accept," cradling the phone. "Alex?" She forced her voice to remain even, ignoring the surge of excitement fluttering in her chest. "You're calling at eleven at night?"

"Yeah," he said, his tone sliding easily through the speaker. "I hope that's not a problem. I just… couldn't stop thinking about today."

A thrill raced through her at the admission. She closed her novel, setting it aside. "Oh. Really?" She tucked her legs under her, suddenly awake. "It was a pretty memorable day, I guess."

"That's one way of putting it. Lunch was… great." His voice sounded deeper than usual, almost soothing in the late-night quiet. "I realized I've never really gotten to talk with you in a relaxed setting— no jog, no chores. It felt nice."

Maia beamed at the memory of sitting across from him in the diner, how he'd listened so attentively. She brushed her fingers over the ring at her necklace. "I loved it, too. I can't stop replaying our conversation," she admitted, warmth creeping into her cheeks. "You… you're different from most people I know."

There was a gentle laugh on the other end of the line. "How so?"

"Well," she said slowly, "people usually put up walls. Even those who are nice don't dig deeper or share much. But you…" She trailed off, her pulse thudding in her ears. "You feel honest. Present."

He paused, and she could sense him smiling. "That means a lot, coming from you. Were you headed to bed?"

She flicked a glance at her novel. "Nah, I was reading a murder mystery—picking up reading again is part of my 'rediscovering my old passions' routine." She giggled softly. "Even though adult life keeps interfering."

Alex chuckled, a low sound that sent a pleasant tingle across her skin. "Funny you say that. I was just thinking about how I used to attend small garage shows, jam out to local bands… and how I've let that go. Phoebe and everything else kind of dulled my spark."

"Maybe you should do it again," Maia said, voice gentle. "Find a way to bring back those parts of yourself."

He inhaled audibly, like her suggestion mattered more than she could guess. "Yeah. You're right. Sometimes, we lose ourselves, and we need a nudge to find the path back."

She smiled, feeling the sweet weight of his sincerity. "Maybe," she whispered. She realized she was gripping the phone tight, fearful of ending the call too soon. "I have to say, I'm grateful we finally exchanged numbers. It's been bugging me how you tried to reach me and I never even knew…"

"Yeah, I wish I'd been smarter about that," Alex said ruefully. "But now I'm glad I can call whenever I can't sleep."

A flutter tugged at her heart. "You couldn't sleep?"

His voice turned softly playful. "Not without saying goodnight. That's all."

Her cheeks felt scalding. She glanced at the time—a few minutes shy of midnight. "Um," she tried, clearing her throat. "We… we have our run in five hours."

"I know," Alex replied. "That's why I was going to let you go. But I just had to hear your voice first."

A warm ache bloomed in her chest. She fought the urge to squeal like a teenager. "Well, you've heard it now. I guess I'll go."

She waited, not wanting to press the button to end. In the silence, she thought she heard him exhale.

"Thank you," he said simply. "For being you."

A flush crept into her cheeks again. "And thank you for being you, too, Alex."

They shared an awkward laugh, and then he softly said, "Goodnight, Maia."

"Goodnight," she whispered, pressing the phone to her ear a moment longer before lowering it. The line cut out, leaving her in the stillness of her bedroom.

She stared at her phone, her heart drumming a frantic rhythm in her chest. *He called me just to say goodnight.* The thought filled her with a quiet, almost reverent joy. She set her phone on the nightstand, then closed her eyes, letting the emotion wash over her.

Everything about Alex—his kindness, his humor, the way he'd stood by her side even when she was at her most vulnerable—told her he might be worth the leap of faith she was so scared to make. Her mind flashed back to his gentle smile, the warmth in his eyes during lunch. If this was what a real second chance at love felt like, maybe she was braver than she thought.

Eventually, she flipped off the lamp, burrowing under the covers. Tomorrow's run promised to be another stepping stone, and she could hardly wait. Warmth and hope mingled inside her, and for once, she welcomed both. Even if the old fear still lurked beneath the surface, Maia Collins was ready to let herself dream again.

CHAPTER SEVENTEEN

Alex sucked in a deep lungful of the cool morning air as he reached the fire hydrant first, halting by its rusted red paint. He glanced back over his shoulder, heart pounding more from anticipation than the run. In the distance, Maia appeared around the corner at the end of the block, her hair bouncing in a high ponytail as she sprinted. Though she still had a decent stretch of sidewalk to go, she pushed forward with determined energy until she finally reached him.

He watched in silent admiration as she bent over, hands braced on her knees, chest rising and falling as she fought to catch her breath. Even when she was gasping for air, there was something about her—maybe her spirit, maybe the way her eyes lit up when she finally lifted her gaze to meet his—that had him feeling unexpectedly protective.

"What? Is it too early for sprinting?" Alex teased, rotating his shoulder to chase away a few knots that had formed during the short run.

His memory slid back to the previous night, recalling how he'd deliberated for a good hour before dialing Maia's number. Calling so late had felt risky—what if he woke her, annoyed her

—but he couldn't help it. He'd wanted to hear her voice, to know more about her day, her life, and the things she held dear. Despite his initial hesitation, the call had felt so right. He'd learned more about her passions, her quirks, and each new piece of information only fueled his desire to keep getting closer. She was slowly becoming... essential.

"No," Maia wheezed, finally managing to speak. "I'm just not used to it." She tilted her face toward the overcast sky, letting her eyes flutter shut. A faint flush crept along her cheeks, either from the run or perhaps from the way Alex looked at her.

Alex tried to hide his concern. He'd suggested this short dash to warm her up for the morning and to share a little adventure together, but maybe he'd overdone it. "How about you take a seat for a second?" he offered, glancing toward several stone stools around a small table in the town's square. "I don't want you keeling over on me."

Maia scoffed good-naturedly. "I'm not that pathetic," she muttered, raising a hand to halfheartedly swipe at him, then narrowed her eyes. "But how are you not tired? Are you a trained athlete or something?"

With that, she began walking again, albeit more slowly, down the sidewalk toward the nearby dance studio—dark windows revealing it wasn't open yet. Main Street was hushed, most businesses still waiting for nine o'clock to roll around. Roasted Beans Coffee Spot and Rochelle's Diner were the only spots lively enough to have flipped their signs to "Open."

Alex shrugged. "I'm no athlete, but I've got a modest gym setup in my living room. Just enough to stay in shape."

Maia let out a small laugh. "Five blocks without breaking a sweat? I'd say that's more than 'just enough.'" She swiped at her brow again, then nudged him playfully. "I'm impressed... and jealous."

He relished the friendly contact of her shoulder bump, already wishing for an excuse to be closer. "Hey, sorry if I pushed you. I just thought a sprint would make up for missing our usual morning jog."

When Maia flashed him a perplexed look, he cleared his throat, shyly tucking his hands into his pockets. "I had an ulterior motive when I suggested we meet early today: I was hoping I could convince you to grab coffee with me."

"Wow. That's one way to do it," she teased, her brown eyes sparkling with amusement. "Ask a girl out for coffee by making her run five blocks first."

"Is that a yes?" Alex asked, masking his sudden nerves with a half-grin.

Maia's lips curved into a sweet smile that nearly knocked the breath out of him more than the sprint had. "Of course it's a yes. Lead the way, Mr. Athlete."

They stopped at the curb, and he gently guided her to pivot toward the inviting glow of Roasted Beans Coffee across the quiet road. He found himself hoping for more moments like this —moments when she'd look at him in that way that made his heart beat a little faster, the slight tilt of her chin letting him know she was having a good time, too.

"You've never been to Roasted Beans?" he asked, a hint of surprise slipping into his tone.

Maia shook her head. "Nope. I'm still so new to Sweetgum that I discover something new almost every day. There's so much this town has to offer."

He liked how close she walked beside him, a gentle sense of companionship in every step. The urge to wrap an arm around her waist flickered in his mind, but he held back, not wanting to rush. Her nearness was enough for now.

Once on the sidewalk, he hurried ahead to open the coffee shop's door before she could. She flashed him a wide, grateful smile, and it was all he could do not to beam like a fool in return.

Maia took a moment in the middle of the small dining area,

inhaling the delicious aroma of freshly ground beans. "Wow… that smell is unreal."

Alex found himself staring at her instead of the place. He'd been here dozens of times, but somehow, seeing her light up over something as simple as the scent of coffee made it all brand-new to him, too. "I know, right?" he said, forcing himself to look away before he got too lost in her expression. "I'd pay good money to learn their secret."

He approached the counter to see if anyone was around, only to find coffee machines, cups, and a glimpse of a storage area in the back. Everything was still.

"I hope we're not barging in before they're ready," Maia murmured, moving closer to his side. Her arm brushed his again—so subtle, yet it made sparks race along his skin.

At that moment, two employees emerged, wearing matching aprons emblazoned with the shop's logo. A tall, friendly-faced man with a name tag reading *Xavier* greeted them first, while a petite woman named *Joanne* joined a beat later, looking slightly frazzled.

"First customers of the day!" Xavier said, a bright smile blooming on his face. "What can I get for you two—besides the honor of being in our coffee kingdom?" He spread his arms theatrically to indicate the décor.

Maia giggled, and Alex appreciated that she was willing to indulge the joke. He still felt a bit curious about what had delayed them in the back, but it didn't seem important now.

"Sorry for the delay," Joanne added, brushing off her apron. "We were tinkering with this new espresso machine. It's supposed to produce a richer brew, but it stalled on us this morning."

"No problem," Alex replied. "So… anything you'd recommend? We're ready for something good."

Both baristas brightened, explaining that they had a new vanilla latte they'd just added to the menu. Alex and Maia exchanged quick, excited looks, deciding almost instantly to try it.

As Joanne disappeared to craft their drinks, Xavier leaned across the counter with a conspiratorial wink. "I see you two were out for an early jog. Good move—burn off the calories before indulging, right?"

Maia nodded. "We weren't just jogging this morning—we sprinted. Isn't that right, Alex?" she asked with playful annoyance.

Alex scratched his head as Xavier laughed. "We won't sprint again if you'd rather not," Alex promised, winking at her.

Xavier pointed at Alex approvingly. "That's the right answer, my guy. Always ensure your partner is comfortable. She comes first at all times—that's my life motto."

Alex couldn't agree more. "I think I'll make it my motto too," he said softly.

Maia glanced at him, her expression unreadable, though Alex thought she looked smitten. *Or maybe I'm just imagining things.* Either way, he liked the reaction.

A moment later, Joanne returned with two steaming cups. She slid them across the counter with a grin. "All right, new policy for this latte: First sip, honest feedback. No sugar-coating."

"Great policy!" Maia said, practically bouncing on her toes as she accepted her cup. She held it out toward Alex, tilting her head. "Cheers?"

He couldn't help the smile tugging at his lips. The morning light streaming in through the window lit her face in a soft glow. "Cheers," he murmured. Their cups touched with a gentle *clink* before they both took their first taste.

Xavier and Joanne leaned forward expectantly, all attention on them.

"Mmm." Maia licked her lips, savoring the velvety notes of vanilla. "This is amazing. I can't believe how smooth it is."

Alex, caught up in watching her reaction, almost forgot to register the flavor. "It's incredible," he agreed, but really, he was thinking *you're incredible*. He took another sip to ground himself. Yes, the latte was good—sweet, but not overpowering. Yet the sweetness in Maia's presence overshadowed it all.

When Maia praised the drink, Joanne exhaled a relieved laugh, and Xavier pumped a triumphant fist. They teased about branding the latte as a "couple's flavor," which made Maia flush lightly. Alex pretended not to notice, but warmth flooded through him.

"Thanks for letting us be your taste testers," Maia said brightly, nodding at Joanne. The atmosphere felt bubbly, like the beginning of something special—and not just because of the coffee.

"We're happy you liked it," Joanne replied. "Feel free to stay and chat or wander around town with your drinks."

Glancing at Alex, Maia tapped her cup. "Let's walk," she suggested, her voice light. "We can sip and enjoy the morning before work calls us back to reality."

Alex nodded, already keen to have her to himself again. "Sounds like a plan."

OUTSIDE, the sky had brightened, revealing a quiet vibrancy along the streets. A few more people milled about now—town residents slowly emerging for the day. Yet somehow, it felt like they remained in their own bubble, sharing a leisurely moment that no one else could interrupt.

Maia talked quickly, animated by the caffeine and her natural zest for conversation. "My favorite part of this new book is the suspense," she confessed, eyes sparkling. "But sometimes I get so anxious, I almost skip to the end. If something bad happens to a character I love, I feel personally betrayed."

Alex chuckled at how seriously she took her fiction. He loved that she was so invested that she felt the story deeply. She happened to be reading a book he had read. "Trust me, I get it. But I'm not giving you any spoilers. You'll thank me later."

She groaned good-naturedly, sipping her latte. "You're such a tease," she said, half serious, half playful. "You keep dropping hints that something big is coming. If a beloved character dies, you need to be prepared to comfort me."

"I can handle a little comforting," Alex joked, though his chest tightened at the thought of holding her in any capacity. "But hey, I didn't say someone dies."

Her eyebrows lifted in challenge, but she let it go. "Fine. Fine. I'll read in tense ignorance."

They drifted past the shops on Main Street, the bright signs and quaint façades reminding Alex of why he'd come back to Sweetgum. There was a warmth here—neighbors who recognized each other, friendly waves, and the comforting sense that this was *home*. He caught sight of a delivery truck pulling up at his parents' restaurant, a reminder of how this small-town life had shaped him. He was proud that Maia was getting a taste of it, too.

When she asked about his recent projects, he thought back to the late nights and the stress of traveling to Atlanta. "It was pretty hectic," he admitted. "But I've heard good feedback. Seeing my work appreciated makes it worth it."

"I can totally relate," Maia said passionately, her words full of conviction about helping her clients. "It's not just about the money, you know?"

He nodded. "You're one of the good ones, Maia," he said softly. It was one of the things that had hooked his attention from the start—her genuine sincerity.

Her cheeks warmed at his praise. "You're pretty great yourself," she countered lightly, eyeing the latte in his hand. "But you drink coffee too slowly. Hurry up, or you'll forget to enjoy it."

Alex chuckled, charmed by her playful scolding. "Watching you enjoy it is enough for me," he answered, the sincerity of his words echoing in his chest. He caught the way her breath seemed to hitch, just for a heartbeat.

"You… you're full of the sweetest words," she said, looking up at him through her lashes.

He swallowed, feeling all sorts of surging emotions swirl inside him. "Wanna do lunch again sometime?" she asked, as if it were the most natural next step.

A broad smile broke across his face. "Or dinner," he suggested, trying to calm the flutter in his stomach.

Her answering grin made the morning sun look dull by comparison. "That sounds wonderful."

They stopped at the edge of the block where a vacant lot opened up beside them, and Alex felt a sudden spike of nerves. Maybe it was time to define this thing between them—was it a date if he asked specifically? They'd shared meals before, but each one felt more significant, like a promise of something deeper.

He cleared his throat. "Maia, would you be open to dinner with me? Just the two of us. I'd really like that."

For a heart-pounding moment, she said nothing. Then her face lit with an enthusiasm that made him feel strangely breathless. "Of course! Tonight? And… where?"

Alex suppressed a relieved laugh. "Yes, tonight. It doesn't have to be anything fancy unless you want it to be."

She waved a hand dismissively. "No need for fancy. As long as it's you and me, it'll be special," she said, her tone turning slightly sultry at the end. It hit him straight in the chest, making his pulse kick up a notch.

A grin tugged at his lips. "Perfect. Maybe we can just grab takeout and do something fun afterward. Keep it… casual." Though the thought of something more romantic flickered in his mind, he loved the idea of a relaxed, private evening, too.

Maia's eyes sparkled at the suggestion. "Where should we meet? My place?"

He considered it briefly, then something more creative popped into his mind. "How about the comic book store? They've got a small lounge area, and sometimes they host themed nights. Could be fun to hang out and geek out—if you're up for it."

She gasped, hands flying to her cheeks. "I had no idea Sweetgum had a comic book store! I'm so in. Yes, please! Pick me up?"

Alex laughed, enamored by her excitement. "Yeah, I'll pick you up. I'll show you all my favorite hidden gems." He glanced at his watch, realizing time was flying. "We should probably head out, though… I don't want your boss deciding to give you mandatory leave again because you're late."

Maia winced comically. "Yikes, you're right. Let's move. I'd like to keep my job."

They made their way down the sidewalk, chatting about possible comics they'd browse later, the takeout they might grab, and all the what-ifs of the evening. The warmth between them felt like a gentle glow, lighting them both from the inside out.

When he finally walked her to her turn-off point, Alex resisted the urge to reach out and brush a stray hair behind her ear. Instead, he offered a simple goodbye that felt heavy with promise. She gave him a cheerful wave, and he lingered a moment, watching her figure retreat, that same comforting flutter in his chest returning.

It wasn't goodbye for long—he'd see her soon.

And that simple fact made his heart soar.

～

ALEX COULD RECOUNT every first with absolute clarity. His first time behind the wheel, first time boarding a plane alone, even his first kiss. The feel of her hand clasped in his, the flush in his cheeks, the scent of sweet perfume lingering on a cool breeze—those memories clung to him like vines.

Now, he was sure he'd never forget how his stomach twisted into an anxious knot on this first dinner date after his divorce. The sense of stepping into something new, so soon after the heartbreak of his past, had a way of sharpening every sensation and emotion.

Standing in front of his mirror, Alex spritzed a little cologne onto his shirt, watching the mist settle onto the black cotton. He checked his reflection: the tension around his eyes had eased. *Is that hope?* He almost didn't recognize himself. It felt surreal—this renewed vibrancy that had been missing for far too long.

He raked his fingers through his hair, wrestling with the stubborn section that always shot straight up. *Stay down,* he silently commanded. Maia might not care if he turned up looking a little disheveled, but she deserved the best version of him. That unshakeable conviction had him smoothing his shirt and straightening his jeans, forcing himself to ignore the fluttering nerves in his gut.

It was only a casual dinner, after all—jeans, sneakers, a crisp black T-shirt. Nothing fancy. Yet it felt like he was preparing for a life-changing moment. *Maybe because you are.*

At six fifty, he slipped his phone into his pocket and forced himself to leave. If he lingered any longer, he'd psych himself out. On the drive to Maia's, the streetlights cast watery reflections on the pavement. His mind buzzed with anticipation. *Don't overthink it... just be yourself.*

His phone vibrated against his thigh as he parked in front of Maia's small, warm-lit home. Glancing at the screen, his heart gave a painful lurch.

Phoebe.

The name alone, glowing starkly in the darkness of the car, made his lungs tighten. Why was she calling now? *You made your choice,* he thought bitterly, sending the call to voicemail with a tap. He rubbed his palm against his thigh, struggling to calm his pulse. *It's over.*

He stepped out of the car and made his way to Maia's door. The crisp night air should have cleared his head, but the ghost of Phoebe's call still hovered. He forced it away. *She won't ruin this night. I won't let her.*

"Coming!" Maia's voice drifted through the door, bright and musical, lifting his spirits instantly. The door swung open, revealing her easy smile and that familiar sparkle in her eyes.

"What's that amazing smell?" she asked, stepping closer. Her gaze fell on his chest, where the scent of his cologne lingered strongest. "Your cologne is heavenly, Alex."

He managed a soft grin, instinctively lowering his head to catch a hint of her own scent: a subtle floral note. *Hold it together,* he told himself, a rush of attraction and sheer relief whipping through him.

"You look incredible, Maia," he said quietly. And she did: her dark green top peeked under an elbow-length jacket, and her jeans hugged her curves just right. Her silver-detailed bag dangled from her shoulder, and her hoop earrings swayed gently every time she tilted her head. "Thanks for agreeing to this. I really… I've been looking forward to tonight."

Her smile widened, and she slipped her arm through his. The warmth of her touch traveled up his forearm, stirring an urge to slide his hand around her waist. But he held back. Not yet—he didn't want to move too fast, not when everything felt this new and precious.

As he walked her to the passenger side of his car and helped her in, the urge intensified, his fingertips tingling at the memory of how it felt to hold a woman close. He swallowed, stepping around to the driver's seat, ignoring his phone's faint buzz. Once they were both buckled in, the radio's soft music filled the intimate space.

"You changed the station," Maia said, half in wonder, swaying her head to the gentle rhythm. "I mentioned this was my favorite band, didn't I?"

"You did," Alex replied, shooting her a quick smile as he reversed onto the street. The phone buzzed again. He glanced down—an email alert, not Phoebe. Relief blossomed in his chest. He let himself exhale, then turned his full attention back to Maia. "I wanted tonight to be perfect. Music is a good place to start."

"It's already perfect," Maia said softly, and the sincerity in her voice made him tighten his grip on the wheel to keep his composure.

During the short drive, she asked about his taste in comics, and he answered with half a mind—his other half was entirely consumed with the feeling of her arm occasionally brushing his, and the near-overwhelming craving to rest his free hand on her knee or twine their fingers together.

He forced himself to stay calm. Wait. Let the moment unfold naturally.

INSIDE THE LOCAL COMIC SHOP, they found an unoccupied table near the back, away from the main shelves. The store's owner, Demetrius, was reading behind the counter, barely looking up to greet them with a wave. They'd pre-ordered dinner from a local fresh-food service, so the savory aroma of chicken, rice, mac and cheese, and vegetables made the small store feel like a cozy bistro.

Alex watched Maia carefully unfold napkins and arrange utensils. Each time she leaned forward, her hair swung across her shoulders, and his gaze lingered there a second too long.

Calm down, man. He tugged at his collar, trying to relieve the heat he felt creeping along his neck.

They ate, made small talk, and soon turned their attention to a brightly colored board game featuring ladders, slides, and cartoonish characters. The store was quiet except for the distant hum of fluorescent lights and the occasional rattle of someone flipping a comic page.

Yet, to Alex, it was as though the world had shrunk to include only Maia—the captivating way she chewed her lip while deciding her next move, the glint in her eye when she teased him, the near-constant laughter that tightened his chest with longing.

"I don't know how you're so good at this," he joked after Maia climbed yet another ladder with her game piece.

She stabbed a piece of chicken and wiggled it victoriously. "I'm a lady of many talents," she said, taking a bite and savoring it.

He had to bite the inside of his cheek to keep from blurting, *And I want to know every one of them.* It was all he could do not to reach across the table and trace a finger along the curve of her hand, or maybe tuck that stray strand of hair behind her ear. But again, he held back.

"Alright," he murmured, rolling the dice with more drama than necessary. "Time for my big comeback."

He got a good roll, and she booed him loudly, her pout so over-the-top that he burst out laughing. "That's a horrible attitude for a champion," he teased, moving his piece up a ladder but still miles behind her on the board.

When she finally trounced him, he held up his hands in defeat, enjoying the sight of her triumphant grin. If losing to her every single time came with that smile, he'd happily lose forever.

They tidied up the game, finishing the last of their meals, and Alex stood, stretching his arms overhead. That subtle movement brought him *too* close to her, and for a heartbeat he wondered if he should let his hand drift to her shoulder. Maybe rub the slight tension out of her neck? His arms ached with the urge, but he stilled them quickly, stepping back.

"Permission to pick which comic we read first?" he asked lightly.

She responded by proposing a little competition: each would pick a comic, and they'd reveal them to each other. She darted off into the shelves, and he jogged in the opposite direction, scanning the spines. The entire time, his heart hammered with excitement and that constant, near-painful desire to just... be *closer* to her.

He returned first, holding a superhero comic. She trailed behind by a few seconds, grumbling under her breath. "You beat me?" she whined good-naturedly.

He chuckled. "Barely."

They read the superhero issue together, flipping through the pages while he gave a dramatic reading of the dialogue. She laughed and offered commentary, occasionally leaning in so close that her shoulder pressed against his, sending jolts of warmth through his veins. Her fragrance—something sweet with a hint of jasmine—kept enveloping him in waves, and it was all he could do not to lean in and inhale.

She's right there, he thought each time she brushed against him. *Just wrap your arm around her. What's stopping you?*

But he resisted, over and over, letting the tension build in him like a coiled spring.

When Maia revealed her own choice—a dark detective comic—she confessed she'd picked it at random. They ended up enthralled by the moody art style and intricate storyline. They made an unspoken pact to buy both comics to keep reading on their own.

THE CAR RIDE back felt electric. Streetlights blurred past, and the hush of late evening draped the town in soft quiet. Maia chatted about the characters, eyes bright, gesturing excitedly. Alex's grip on the steering wheel was tighter than ever, not from caution but from the raw tension in his muscles—he could practically feel the heat of her presence in the passenger seat.

When he pulled up in front of her home, the porch light illuminated them both. He climbed out, circling to open her door, and as she stood, the space between them practically fizzled with unspoken possibility.

God, I want to touch her.

They strolled up her walkway side by side, and Alex's pulse thundered. Each time he brushed her hand accidentally, adrenaline spiked, making him want to tangle his fingers with hers. Still, he held back. *Not yet. Don't rush...*

Standing at her door, Maia turned to face him. She clasped her hands behind her, leaning in slightly. The light overhead caught the shine in her eyes. He had the wild impulse to cup her cheek, to let his thumb trace that gentle curve from her lips to her jawline, to see if her skin felt as soft as it looked.

"Tonight was so fun," she said, voice quiet, an affectionate smile on her lips. "I love doing things like this—trying new places, seeing new sides of the same old town. Doing it with you made it extra special."

Alex's heart squeezed. "I feel the same," he managed, mouth suddenly dry. "It's been a while since I've... since I've enjoyed an evening like this."

She nodded, understanding reflecting in her gaze. "We should do it again soon."

He reached into his pocket, recalling the email he'd gotten earlier. "Actually... there's a work event in Atlanta. A cocktail dinner to celebrate the ad campaign. They said I can bring a plus one, and I—I'd really like it if you'd come with me."

Her face lit up, and that single expression felt like the

brightest thing he'd seen in years. "I'd love that!" she said eagerly, fiddling with her keys. "Do we really have to wait until next week?"

Her enthusiasm loosened something inside his chest, making him laugh—pure, easy. "If I had my way, I'd take you out again tomorrow."

They stood there a moment longer, neither moving to go inside. Alex was hyper-aware of the inches between them—only inches! He could so easily bridge the gap, capture her mouth in a gentle kiss. His body practically ached with that longing. Instead, he smiled.

"Good night, Maia," he said softly, voice rough with suppressed tension.

"Good night, Alex," she replied, giving him a look that said she sensed the same tension too—and maybe, just maybe, was waiting for him to make the move.

He didn't. He let her unlock her door, step inside, and wave goodbye. He turned around slowly, heart pounding, every part of him on fire with yearning he couldn't quite bring himself to act upon. *Patience,* he chided himself. *Next time.*

Back at his own house, the phone glowed with a missed call and a voicemail—Phoebe's. He stared at it for a long moment, then shook his head. *That's the past.*

Without listening, he deleted the message. His chest felt light, and for the first time in a long while, the weight of those old memories shifted.

His thoughts drifted back to Maia—the way she smelled, the warmth of her laughter, how his entire body had strained to hold her. *This is a first I'll remember just as vividly,* he realized. *And I can't wait for what comes next.*

CHAPTER EIGHTEEN

Maia's skin prickled with goosebumps. It wasn't just the cool night air; it was the way Alex's eyes sparkled beneath the faint light of the stars. Their silver glow reflected in his deep brown irises, making him seem even more alive, more open. Compared to the guarded man she'd first met, he looked brighter now—like a weight had lifted off his shoulders.

She liked to think she'd had some part in that transformation. And if she was honest, he'd transformed her too. He filled her days—and nights—with a sense of hope, making her feel like she could be fearless again. She hoped he felt the same.

Tonight marked their third dinner in a single week. On paper, these meals had been a kind of "practice" for the upcoming gala, but there was no denying the truth: *They simply wanted to be together.*

Now, here they stood under the small arch of her porch, drenched in warm light from the nearby fixture. Alex lingered by her door with an air of hesitation, as though he were reluctant to leave. She curled her fingers around the key in her hand, her heart skipping every time she glanced at him.

"I'm sure we'll have a great time," he said gently, his voice low and hushed. He flicked his gaze to his car parked at the curb.

"When?" Maia asked, tilting her head.

"The gala," Alex clarified, though his tone trembled slightly, as if part of him feared she'd forgotten or changed her mind.

Maia's heart softened; she pressed a comforting hand to his arm. "I'm certain I'll have fun there. Just like I've had fun tonight, and the night before that, and the one before *that*." She allowed a warm smile to overtake her face. "Every dinner we've had has been... amazing."

Alex's eyes flickered with a mix of hope and doubt. He glanced away, swallowing as though words were caught in his throat.

Sudden anxiety tugged at Maia's chest. *Did I say too much? Am I coming on too strong?* Doubts swirled in her mind. "I—"

"Sorry," Alex interrupted, rubbing the back of his neck. A sheepish grin curved his lips. "I'm being awkward. I just... I don't really want this night to end."

A heady relief washed over Maia, making her laugh aloud. "Oh, thank goodness! I thought I was the only one wishing we could make the hours stretch forever."

Her words seemed to lighten him. He shifted a little closer, his hand drifting near her waist before stopping short. She saw the longing in his eyes—a sudden desire to close the distance, balanced by that same lingering hesitation.

"We need to work on saying what we feel more often," he murmured, eyes locked on hers. "Who knows how many times we've both felt the same thing but stayed quiet?"

A pleasurable warmth swept through her as she realized how near he was. The faint scents of cologne and fresh night air wrapped around her senses. She almost shivered from the awareness coursing through her body—he was so close she could pick out each fleck of gold in his irises.

"Well, we could start right now," she said, voice a little breathier than usual. "Right now, I'm happy to welcome you into my home." She raised her chin toward the door. "If you want to come in."

A radiant smile broke across his face. "I'm happy to be invited."

They stepped inside, and Maia was more keenly aware of him than ever before. She caught the light brush of his fingertips against her shoulder as he moved past her, careful not to jostle her. That small contact alone sent sparks dancing through her veins.

"I had a really good time tonight," Maia confessed, leading him into the kitchen. Her pulse still fluttered from the simple act of letting him cross her threshold.

"So did I," Alex replied, leaning against the counter when she flipped on the light.

Without thinking too hard, she grabbed two bottles of beer from the fridge. The little hiss of carbonation punctuated the silence. She handed one to Alex, holding up hers in a playful toast. "To being on the same page."

His bottle clinked against hers. "To being on the same page," he echoed. That small gesture felt like a promise, and the intensity of his gaze made her entire body tingle.

Maia sipped her drink, eyes sweeping down Alex's throat as he swallowed. She'd never been aware of something as simple as a man's neck before, but now, every detail had her heart picking up speed. *Don't stare,* she warned herself, turning her head a fraction. *He might notice.*

Alex took another sip before setting his bottle on the counter, drawing her full attention back to him. "And what if tonight… I don't know… leads us into the morning?"

There it was. Out in the open. The simple question somehow lit a bonfire of nerves and anticipation in her stomach. She swirled the cool glass in her hand, a coy smile tugging at her lips. "Then so be it," she said softly. "We'll just do our usual routine—get up, run the block... like we do every morning."

He laughed, and the sound settled warmly in her chest. "That's true." His eyes held a meaning that made heat pool low in her belly.

She wanted to close the distance, but she kept the conversation light. "I think we'll manage," she teased, raising her bottle in a mock toast again. *Yes, I definitely want him to stay.*

They lapsed into a comfortable silence as they finished the beers. Alex was first to speak, a thoughtful note in his voice. "You know, this is the happiest I've felt since coming back to Sweetgum."

Her smile faltered slightly at the raw honesty in his tone. "Why haven't you been happy?" she asked, setting her nearly empty bottle aside.

He exhaled, the tension in his expression telling her how difficult the memories were. "I've been stuck in my head for a long time. My mom kept urging me to go out, to let myself enjoy life again. But after the divorce, it's hard to believe you deserve anything good."

Maia nodded, her own past heartbreak flaring to life. She gently rested her hand on his forearm, her thumb tracing a reassuring line on his sleeve. "I get it. I've felt worthless before too... Rejection does that to people."

He nodded slowly, the kitchen light catching on the edges of his hair. "Especially when everything ends badly. You start blaming yourself... thinking about all the arguments, all the red flags you overlooked until they exploded in your face."

The pain in his voice pulled at her heart. "Same," she whispered. "After everything fell apart, I couldn't shake the feeling that I'd done something *horribly* wrong. But then I realized there were problems all along. Problems I kept ignoring."

Alex gave a wry laugh. "We fought so much, neighbors

started knocking on our door to intervene. Someone called the cops once, and I realized… we were beyond fixing. I tried to make it work, but by then, she was already halfway out the door."

Maia's throat tightened. She couldn't imagine how that must have felt. Slowly, she laced her fingers through his, heart pounding as she took the risk of that physical closeness. "Sometimes," she said, "I think fate has other plans for us."

He squeezed her hand softly, and that simple pressure felt like a lifeline. "It does. I'm glad I finally listened." The weight in his voice faded, replaced by warmth as he looked at her.

Maia felt an electric jolt of hope. "Would you like to sit?" She managed a lopsided smile, trying to lighten the mood.

In a few moments, they were side by side on her soft, worn couch, shoes off and legs tucked up. The overhead light cast a gentle glow across the room, enough to see each other's expressions clearly. She asked him about high school, teased him about outrunning athletes. He teased her right back, calling her "wildly talented" for beating him at every board game they played. Their laughter bounced off the walls, warming the space until it felt like a cocoon.

"Okay, serious question," Maia said eventually, hugging a throw pillow to her chest. "Why didn't you go pro? With all that running skill, you could've been an Olympian."

Alex snorted, draping his arm along the back of the couch, just inches from her shoulder. "Sports aren't my real passion. I can join a casual game, but that's all."

Her gaze flitted to his bicep, momentarily distracted by how close he was. "So then… what's your dream?" she asked. "Become the king of ad campaigns across the country?"

He laughed, raking a hand through his hair. "Not exactly. My dream is simpler: to make my family proud, to help with the restaurant if needed. Keep up my freelancing in a way that supports them if they retire."

A wave of affection rolled through Maia. *He's so genuine.* "That's beautiful," she said softly.

"What about you?" he asked, eyes searching her face. "Where do you see yourself?"

She exhaled, letting the pillow slip from her arms. "I want to be happy," she admitted. "I want to take care of myself—and if I'm lucky, share that happiness with someone who cares just as much."

A charged silence hung between them. Slowly, Alex lifted his hand from the couch, lightly grazing her cheek. His touch was warm, steady, and her entire body buzzed with the sweetest tension.

"I like you, Maia," he said, his tone low, sincere. "I like how you talk to me, how you make me feel… I want more of it. I want more of *you*."

Her breath caught in her throat. She placed her hand over his, feeling the faint tremor in his fingers. "Same page?"

"Same page," he whispered.

Then he leaned in, and Maia met him halfway. Their lips brushed in a tentative kiss, gentle yet brimming with anticipation. A pleasant dizziness seized her as he threaded his fingers into her hair. His kiss felt like a promise, like an acknowledgment of everything they'd shared—and everything they still hoped for.

Time blurred. Soft, tentative kisses melted into deeper ones, each exchange of breath pulling them closer. She sensed his hesitation melding with need, the gentle way he cradled her face telling her he wasn't going anywhere—and neither was she.

Heart pounding, she shifted, sliding onto his lap so she could kiss him with more abandon. He responded instantly, hands splaying across her waist and shoulders as though he had to touch her everywhere at once. Maia let out a soft sound in the back of her throat, the sensation of being cherished and desired making her dizzy.

Eventually, they paused, foreheads pressed together, breath mingling. She opened her eyes to find him watching her with a look that made her chest clench—in the best possible way.

He stood, lifting her effortlessly, and she let out a little laugh of surprise as she wrapped her legs around his waist for balance. "My room," she whispered between smiles, trying to contain the flutter of nerves and excitement. "Upstairs."

With another kiss, Alex carried her toward the steps. Somewhere between kisses, they paused just long enough for Maia to whisper directions. From there, instinct took over, and nothing else mattered but the two of them.

BIRDSONG STIRRED MAIA AWAKE. The gentle light of early morning spilled through the gap in her curtains, illuminating the man next to her in a glow that felt almost unreal. *He's here.* Warmth spread through her chest at the sight of Alex sleeping, his hair adorably mussed, the sheets sliding just below his chest. She studied the faint lines of muscle across his shoulders, the peaceful expression on his face.

I could get used to this.

Tentatively, she reached out, letting her fingers graze the soft strands of his hair. She still couldn't believe how right everything felt—physically, yes, but also emotionally. Last night, he'd shown her in so many ways that she was seen, appreciated, and, in a sense, protected. It was a feeling she'd all but given up on.

Her gaze drifted down to the small ring dangling from the chain around her neck—her symbol of past wounds she'd never fully let go. She touched it absentmindedly, her mind swirling with renewed certainty: *She didn't need that crutch anymore.*

Alex's eyes opened, blinking away sleep. He turned his head, and a slow smile spread across his face. "Hey," he said in a hushed morning rasp.

Warmth flooded Maia's cheeks. "Morning," she whispered. "Sleep well?"

"Better than I have in a long time," he murmured, propping himself on one elbow and glancing around her room as though committing it to memory. His eyes flicked back to her, and he reached out, brushing a stray curl behind her ear. "I could get used to *this*," he added with a grin.

A pleasant shiver traveled down her spine. Unable to hide her giddiness, Maia fiddled with the ring on her necklace. But as her fingers toyed with it, she felt a shift in her chest—like she was finally ready to put the past to rest.

Alex noticed her pause. "What is it?"

She inhaled, heart thudding, then unfastened the clasp. She slipped the ring and chain off in one fluid motion and set them carefully in the drawer of her bedside table. "I don't think... I need it anymore," she explained. Saying it made her feel both nervous and euphoric.

Alex's gaze softened, understanding shining in his eyes. "Are you sure?" he asked gently.

She nodded. "I held onto it for so long—because I was scared, uncertain. But not anymore." A soft smile curved her lips. "I'm finally ready to let it go."

He leaned in, pressing a tender kiss to her forehead. "Same page," he whispered against her skin.

Her heart fluttered wildly at those simple words. *Yes. We truly are on the same page now.*

They slid out of bed, and Maia grabbed a robe while Alex gathered his clothes. She gave him a small grin, taking pleasure in the comfortable intimacy as he pulled on yesterday's shirt. "Let me show you the bathroom," she said, leading him down the hall.

❤ 153 ❤

LESS THAN AN HOUR LATER, they were side by side in her kitchen, the sun fully up and streaming through the windows. Both of them agreed to forgo their usual morning run—something about the coziness of the moment made them reluctant to let it end.

"You wouldn't think a dash of almond essence would work in eggs, but it does," Alex said confidently, whisking the mixture in a small bowl.

Maia arched an eyebrow, chuckling as she took out the blender for smoothies. "Almond essence in eggs? Are you sure?" She seemed skeptical, but the gentle aroma filling the air made her mouth water. "Alright, Mr. Food Connoisseur. Impress me."

Alex just grinned, transferring the whisked eggs into a hot pan. "My parents own a restaurant, remember? I've absorbed a thing or two."

"So… your talents extend to cooking as well." Maia teased. She dropped some frozen berries, yogurt, and milk into the blender, hitting the switch. The machine roared to life, momentarily drowning out their laughter.

In moments, Alex killed the heat under the pan, plating the golden, fragrant eggs with surprising finesse. Maia poured two glasses of smoothie, placing them on the small kitchen table he'd cleared off.

She settled into a chair, heart fluttering when Alex pulled it out for her before taking a seat across from her. It was a simple, domestic gesture, but her chest warmed at his thoughtfulness.

"You know," he said, "if you're ever interested in learning a more complex dish, I'd love to show you." He shot her a playful look as he dished some of the eggs onto her plate.

"Yes, please," Maia replied eagerly, taking a forkful. The flavor burst across her tongue, and she let out a small hum of approval. "Wow… This is *amazing*."

They dug into breakfast, exchanging contented smiles. Somewhere between sips of her smoothie and compliments about Alex's cooking, Maia felt a profound sense of rightness. *This was real.*

Despite all the pain and fear that used to surround her, Maia felt the last of those barriers slip away. She reached across the table, her fingertips grazing his wrist. When he looked up, their eyes locked in a silent exchange of understanding.

"You ready for the next part of this journey?" he asked quietly, voice filled with hope.

Maia squeezed his hand, a sure smile gracing her lips. "Absolutely," she said. She was ready—ready to trust him, to believe in a shared future, to embrace what the world offered them both.

And as she watched him smile back, she knew: *They were on the same page, and there was no turning back.*

CHAPTER NINETEEN

"Zip me?" Maia called out, her fingertips balanced lightly on her waist.

Aimee dropped her phone onto the tangle of half-rejected outfits piled on Maia's bed and stepped over. The faint whirr of the zipper moving up sent a small thrill through Maia, and she turned to face her mirror. The striking red dress hugged every curve from her bust to her knees, while her tallest black heels gave her a confidence boost she usually lacked. She hoped the outfit would strike the right note for a formal event—*elegant* but not over-the-top.

Aimee's eyes shone with approval. "Look at you!" she said, beaming. "Mrs. Zhang is going to dazzle them tonight. I'm sure Alex will be proud to have you as his plus one." She snatched her phone from the bed, pointing it at Maia.

"Aimee—" Maia groaned, knowing what was coming. Her friend snapped a quick photo anyway. Maia exhaled, adjusting the hem of her dress as though that might somehow shield her from the camera. "Don't call me that! Alex and I have been officially dating for, what, a month?" She paused, eyes flicking to the reflection of her lips as she pressed them together to even out her lipstick. "Hardly enough time to start calling me his wife."

Aimee's skeptical look said it all.

Maia shrugged, smoothing the dress once more. "I'm *just* his girlfriend," she mumbled, voice warming at the idea. "His girlfriend who… kind of sees him almost every day." Even saying the word "girlfriend" triggered a little flutter in her stomach. Their relationship had been a whirlwind of texts, calls, and hours spent sharing stories she'd never shared with anyone else.

She raised her left wrist and let the charms on her bracelet jingle: a tiny shoe, a miniature blueberry, and a small metal novel. That one piece of jewelry made her happier than anything else in her closet. Derek's old gifts might have been shiny and expensive, but they hadn't meant *anything* like these charms did. Alex's gift felt personal—like he knew exactly who she was.

Aimee set her hands on her hips. "Listen, don't say 'just his girlfriend' like it's nothing." She reached out, turning Maia by the shoulders so they were face-to-face. "Girl, you tell that man everything, and the two of you are practically glued at the hip. If that's not serious, I don't know what is."

Maia let out an incredulous laugh. "Am I neglecting you? We still have our dinners." She moved to her bed and scooped up the sleek black handbag she'd decided on for the gala. It rested among the other bags she'd modeled for Aimee earlier—rejects scattered around. She'd deal with that mess once she got home.

Aimee clasped her hands beneath her chin, batting her lashes as though smitten. "You could never neglect me. I *like* hearing about your grand adventures with Alex—makes me feel all fuzzy inside. Besides, I'm fine with just one dinner a week if it means you're spending every other night with the love of your life." She punctuated her teasing with a dramatic string of air-kisses.

Maia gave a short laugh, the warmth building inside her. "I

didn't say he's the love of my life. You're the one throwing words around like that." She watched herself in the mirror again, noticing how her glossy black clutch looked right at home against the vivid red dress. Would Alex think she looked beautiful? He told her that every day, but this time it felt extra special —like she wanted to *prove* him right.

Derek had been thoughtful once, but never this consistent. Alex, on the other hand, *never* missed a morning text or call— not even if they were about to jog together in an hour. They chatted through mundane things and big confessions alike, and she felt fully seen every time. It was so different, so *new*… and so exhilarating.

"You *love* him," Aimee said, arching an eyebrow decisively. "How can you not? You're totally smitten. From what you say, he's basically obsessed with you in the same way. If that's not love, then I'm clueless."

Maia swallowed, letting her handbag dangle from her fingertips. *Could she really be that obvious?* The last month had sped by in a haze of laughter, mutual support, and easy companionship. She shared more with Alex in casual conversations than she'd ever shared in her previous marriage. With Derek, her answers had slowly shrunk to one-word replies, but with Alex… she could talk for hours. *Or just listen to his voice and be content.*

She stroked the blueberry charm on her bracelet, a subtle wave of warmth rolling through her at the memory of how he'd chosen it specifically—blueberries from their first early-morning diner date. A small, thoughtful detail, yet it represented so much. "I don't know," she whispered. "It just seems too soon."

Aimee took a step closer, raising her eyes to Maia's. "Maia, love doesn't show up on some schedule. It happens when it happens."

Maia let the thought sink in. She'd never felt so comfortable, so unguarded with another person—even with Derek. Alex gave her the space to be independent, yet supported her whenever she needed it. She didn't feel helpless without him; rather, she *chose* to be with him because he made everything brighter. Wasn't that the ultimate sign of love?

Before she could say anything else, her phone buzzed on the cluttered dresser. Seeing **Alex** on the screen sent a thrill through her chest. Aimee's eyes danced knowingly, but Maia waved her down.

"Hey," Maia answered softly, trying not to let the surge of excitement bleed too obviously into her voice.

Aimee hopped in place, hands clasped tight in glee.

Maia turned her back slightly. "Yeah, I'm ready," she murmured, after Alex said he was outside. "I'll be right there."

She hung up, and Aimee followed her to the door, grinning. "You go, Mrs. Zhang," she teased again in a sing-song voice, prompting Maia to shush her, though she couldn't hide her smile.

Outside, the air was crisp, laced with the subtle scent of pine from the trees along the sidewalk. The sky was soft with dusk, and a hush blanketed the neighborhood. Maia spotted Alex's car by the curb, his headlights illuminating the patch of road in front of him.

As she approached, he climbed out. Instantly, her pulse kicked up; *goodness,* he looked incredible. His dark blue suit caught the light in a gentle shimmer, a white button-up visible beneath, and a slim black tie to pull it all together. Even his shoes gleamed. She found her fingertips itching to brush along the neat lapels, just to confirm he was real.

He opened the passenger door with a courteous flourish. "Ready to go?" he asked, gaze roaming appreciatively over her dress. A slow smile tipped his lips, and Maia felt that familiar warmth rush through her.

"I definitely am," she replied, settling into the seat. The quiet hum of the engine surrounded her, along with the hint of Alex's cologne—a subtle, woodsy note that made her want to lean in. She clicked on her seatbelt, then added, "And... *wow*. You look amazing. Seriously."

Alex's smile broadened. "Thank you. You look like a movie star tonight." There was an unmistakable note of pride in his tone. He closed the door behind her gently, then rounded the hood of the car to slide into the driver's seat.

The moment he pulled away from the curb, Maia risked a sideways glance. In the glow of the dash lights, Alex looked both focused and relaxed, a confident ease in how he turned the wheel. It struck her again how *natural* it felt to be with him.

A thousand unspoken words floated through her mind, the strongest being *I love you*. She silently wondered if he felt the same. Perhaps he did, but neither of them seemed ready to voice it—*yet*. At least, not tonight. Not on a night when Alex had something important to attend, something that showcased his hard work.

The warm flutter in her chest told her the words were there, waiting for the right moment. Until then, she savored the quiet closeness, the mutual smiles, and the knowledge that this was only the beginning of something extraordinary.

CHAPTER TWENTY

He'd never seen so many works of art in one place.

A gentle hush blanketed the museum's top-floor exhibition room, punctuated by low conversations and the clink of champagne glasses. Under the warm overhead lights, vibrant paintings and intricate sculptures lined every wall, each piece radiant and compelling in its own way. Alex couldn't help but marvel at the array—abstract shapes bursting with color, lifelike portraits that seemed to breathe, statues capturing human grace in cold marble.

So far, the night had gone remarkably well. An enthusiastic museum employee had greeted him and Maia at the main entrance and then escorted them up to this lofty gallery. Through glass-paneled walls and grand staircases, they'd passed mesmerizing exhibits on every floor. By the time they reached the top, the long climb felt satisfying, like they'd earned the right to see the "crown jewels" of the show.

The event itself was a grand soirée organized by Intersect Inc. to celebrate the success of Alex's ad campaign. Familiar faces from the business world floated around the space—names he'd only heard of until now but recognized instantly: CEOs in sleek suits, marketers in elegant dresses, all mingling with the kind of assuredness that came with power. Had he been here alone, Alex might have felt out of place or even intimidated. But Maia's steady presence beside him chased away that tension.

She'd navigated the crowd as if she'd done this a thousand times. Every new introduction seemed effortless for her. With her warm smile and engaging questions, she ensured no conversation faltered. People gravitated toward her, drawn by her approachable nature and confident composure. Alex watched in awe, occasionally chiming in but mostly letting Maia take the lead. Whenever he felt his energy wane from constant chatter, a quick glance at her face—at those shining eyes and that soft, encouraging smile—was all it took to remind him why he was here.

And she looked absolutely stunning tonight. The red dress fit her like a dream, making Alex proud to call her his date—though he realized, with a heady rush, that *date* didn't begin to capture what they really were to each other. At least, not in his heart.

The evening slipped past in a haze of introductions, polite laughter, and art appreciation. By nine p.m., a specialty brand of champagne was poured and distributed. The pop of corks, followed by a wave of clinking glasses, announced the night's celebratory toast. Alex took a sip, finding the taste both slightly bitter and strangely refreshing. The light buzz it left him with felt… freeing.

Now, nearly two hours later, the crowd had begun to thin. Musicians in the far corner continued to play a soft, lilting melody, and the staff discreetly tidied away empty glasses. Alex walked beside Maia down a wide corridor leading to the elevator. They'd said their goodbyes to colleagues and acquaintances moments before, and each step they took away from the main gallery brought a renewed sense of quiet. The echo of their footsteps on polished marble added to the hush, giving this part of the museum an almost sacred quality.

In truth, Alex felt beyond grateful for the lull. As much as he could summon charm when needed, his introverted nature craved these peaceful moments to recharge. Maia, on the other hand, seemed to effortlessly glide through social settings. He marveled at how she'd engaged with everyone from top executives to art curators, never missing a beat. Over the course of the evening, he'd come to rely on her uncanny knack for knowing when to step in and when to give him a reprieve.

He allowed his attention to wander briefly, soaking in the details of the corridor: gold-framed paintings shimmering under spotlights, the faint hum of air-conditioning, the distant echo of a final group of guests chatting somewhere behind them. Despite the hour, the museum's bright lighting kept the space far from eerie. *Quite the opposite,* Alex thought. It was romantic, a bit like a private tour they had all to themselves.

He glanced at Maia. With each swing of her hair, he thought about how he'd felt when they first met—unsure, guarded. Now, she was the reason he no longer felt like a stranger here. Even in this grand setting, with all these powerful people, he belonged— because Maia was by his side.

An image of her laughing earlier that night flickered across his mind. She'd been listening to a marketing executive's long-winded story, yet she'd managed to find genuine humor in his anecdotes. That laugh had tugged at Alex's heart. *I love her,* he thought. And the moment he did, his heart jolted as if he'd caught himself stepping off a ledge. *Love.* It was the same word that had lingered for weeks, refusing to leave him alone.

Could he really be in love with Maia so soon after his painful divorce? Doubt gnawed at him, but it was overwhelmed by the simple truth—*she made him feel alive again.* She made everything seem possible. Maybe it was ill-advised, maybe it was faster than he'd expected, but he couldn't deny his feelings any longer.

His palms felt clammy at the realization. He wiped them discreetly against his pants. *What if she doesn't feel the same?* Or worse, *what if she's not ready to hear it?* This was uncharted territory for him—opening himself up after heartbreak, daring to hope that a new love could blossom in the aftermath.

They passed a gallery of impressionist paintings. The brushstrokes blurred together, vibrant colors melding into soft illusions of figures and landscapes. It reminded him of how he'd felt about Maia at first: an appealing swirl of color he hadn't fully understood. But now he saw her more clearly, every distinct detail—her kindness, her intelligence, her passion. She was no longer an abstract concept but a tangible force in his life.

He slowed his pace, taking a breath. *This is it*, he told himself. *Tell her.* The corridor was empty, bathed in quiet. The overhead lights glowed softly, and the hush gave everything a hush of intimacy. If there was a moment to confess how he felt, this was surely it.

Just as he opened his mouth, Maia turned to him, her expression suddenly more serious than he'd seen all night. "Alex?" she asked, her voice hushed.

He stopped cold, heart tripping. She *looked* worried, or at least a little anxious. Did she sense his internal shift?

"Yes?" he managed, blood pounding in his ears.

"We need to talk."

Those four words froze him where he stood. He swallowed, forcing himself not to panic. After such a lovely evening, *what could be weighing on her mind?* A knot of dread coiled in his stomach, battling the flutter of hope he'd felt only moments ago. *Please let this be good news,* he silently prayed.

He steadied himself and stepped closer, bracing for whatever might come next.

CHAPTER TWENTY-ONE

A faint echo of footsteps trailed behind them in the corridor, but Maia and Alex stood wrapped in quiet, apart from the bustle of the gala. The hum of air-conditioning blew softly against her shoulders, and the muted glow of recessed lights made the polished floor gleam. Everything in this museum radiated grandeur and sophistication. Yet at that moment, Maia's only focus was on Alex.

She swallowed hard, feeling the weight of her words pressing on her chest. "We need to talk," she'd blurted. *God, what a horrible start.* The phrase sounded so final, like an ominous warning siren. It was the same set of words she'd used in the past to deliver terrible news—and she knew, from Alex's startled look, how he must have taken it. *He looks ready to run.*

"Wait, no," she stumbled, raising her free hand as if that might physically reel back the dread. She caught sight of tension in Alex's brow.

"Everything okay?" he asked, reaching out to touch her elbow. His fingers were light, but that gentle contact made warmth spread through her.

Maia's purse strap dug into her palm from how tightly she

was gripping it. She wanted to speak, to assure him everything was fine—better than fine—but the words stuck in her throat. An irrational fear roared up, the old fear of loving someone who didn't love her back.

Before she could force out an explanation, Alex's touch shifted. He gently guided her to turn toward the wall. "Look," he said, voice quiet yet firm.

Maia directed her gaze to the painting before them. At first glance, it appeared to be a swirl of colors—smears of bright orange, cool blues, greens, and bold splashes of yellow. The longer she stared, the more it came into focus: it could be a planet, or a sunflower, or a spinning universe. Each possibility shimmered in the shifting patterns of paint.

"I hadn't even noticed this," she murmured, allowing herself a moment to fully absorb the swirling hues.

Alex folded his arms over his chest, taking in the painting with her. His presence was steady and calm. For a moment, they stood there together, letting the hypnotic patterns of color siphon off the tension that had been building.

After a few measured breaths, Maia realized the anxiety that had clutched her throat had loosened considerably. She let out a short laugh, almost in disbelief. "It's strange, but I do feel better."

Alex's arm curved around her shoulders as he leaned in. "Art has a way of distracting me, too," he said. "Sometimes, all we need is to focus on something beautiful until our mind clears." His voice dipped low, a gentle hush meant just for her. "Whatever you have to say, I'm here to listen. I don't want you to be scared. Not with me."

That last phrase sent a soft flutter coursing through her whole body. *Not with me.* For an instant, she imagined life as it could be—someone who'd stand by her, encourage her, share her burdens. As if to emphasize how safe she was, he pressed a tender kiss to her forehead. Maia nearly melted into him, letting her purse slide down her arm until she clutched it at her side.

"Okay," she breathed, stepping back a fraction so she could look up at him. The overhead lights highlighted the earnest concern in his eyes. She searched for the right opener, the perfect metaphor that might gently lead into the confession swirling inside her chest. Her heart hammered, adrenaline buzzing in her veins.

She drew in a slow breath. "Do you remember that song I made you listen to? The one from my high school days—the one about how life is this wild roller coaster ride?"

A faint smile appeared on his face. "Of course. The lyrics about the sharp turns and loop-the-loops… can't forget them."

His voice—warm and attentive—felt like the sweetest invitation. Maia smiled in return, feeding off the kindness she saw there. "You always pay attention," she said, a gentle astonishment weaving through her words. *He pays attention to every detail, big or small.* "Well… that's how I feel about meeting you. About us. It's like I stepped onto this roller coaster and you were already buckled in next to me. I couldn't get off if I tried."

She paused, letting that imagery sink in. His gaze stayed steady, reflecting a mix of encouragement and anticipation.

"I guess what I'm trying to say is…" She exhaled shakily, then pressed onward, voice trembling with emotion. "I love you, Alex. I know it's only been a few months, but I… I can't ignore what's been building inside me. You complement me in ways nobody else has. I fantasize about a future with you. And I don't want to pretend I'm not falling for you… hard."

There—the confession was out. Relief and terror twined together in her chest. Now she had to wait for his reaction. Her heart thumped an erratic beat.

For a moment, he simply stared at her, his lips parted in astonishment. Then, in a burst of sound that startled her, Alex tipped his head back and *cackled*. It wasn't a mocking laugh— more like a giddy, unrestrained outpouring of joy. But still, seeing him laugh like that made her chest tighten with confusion.

"Alex?" she said, worry edging her voice. Had she broken him?

He only took a few seconds to compose himself, broad grin still in place. Without warning, he tugged her into his arms, enveloping her in a warm, secure hug. Maia's face pressed against his chest, and she breathed in the faint traces of his cologne. *He's hugging me... so this is good, right?*

When he pulled back, there was a gleam in his eye she'd never seen before—radiant, almost carefree. He pressed another quick kiss to her forehead, and she felt her fear drain away.

She managed a small laugh, fueled by relief. "What is going on with you? I've never seen you laugh like that."

"Maia…" He cradled her face with both hands, gently. "I love you too," he said, words rolling out in a rush. "I've been wrestling with how to tell you. I was so scared it was too soon, that you'd think I was out of my mind. And here you are, telling me first."

Maia's heart soared so high she felt dizzy. A bubbling sense of pure happiness rushed through her, making her want to dance or jump into his arms. She couldn't fight the gleaming smile overtaking her face. "You really do?"

His eyes sparkled. "I swear," he whispered. "I've never felt this way about anyone. I've been trying to find a perfect moment to confess, but… I guess we sort of created it tonight."

She flung her arms around his neck, and he gathered her into a tighter embrace. For a few long seconds, they just stood there, holding each other like they might fuse into one person. The low hum of the museum's lights buzzed overhead, but inside Maia's heart, it felt like a silent symphony was playing.

Eventually, Alex loosened his hold and guided her gently down the corridor, his arm still draped around her shoulders in a comforting, possessive way. "I have to admit," he said, letting out a breathy chuckle, "when you started talking with those dreaded 'we need to talk' words, I thought I was about to get the worst news."

Maia grimaced at her own phrasing. "I know. That was so clumsy. Honestly, if you had said that to me, I would've panicked, too." She laced her fingers with his, enjoying how his larger hand enveloped hers. "I'm sorry for scaring you, but… I had to get your attention. I was so nervous."

Alex gave her a fond, lopsided grin and squeezed her hand lightly. "I guess fate has a sense of humor, letting us both freak out before we realized we feel the exact same way." His expression softened. "But seriously… I've been through a divorce, so those words just set off every alarm bell in my head."

Understanding flooded Maia, and she rested her cheek against his shoulder as they walked. "I get it. I've been there, too." A little pang of sadness flickered in her chest, remembering that old pain—but it vanished the moment she looked up to see his tender smile again. "Luckily, we don't have to worry about that right now."

He turned his head toward her, eyes shining. "No. Not at all," he murmured. "Thank you for reminding me that there's still so much good in life. You… you've helped me remember how to hope for more."

Warmth flowed through her, from her chest outward. She paused in their slow steps, turning to face him fully. "I'm glad," she said, voice thick with emotion.

They gazed at each other, the hush of the museum making the moment feel strangely intimate, as if the world beyond them had stopped turning. In that gaze, Maia realized she had never felt so safe, so *wanted*. The current of understanding between them was almost tangible, wrapping them in a cocoon of mutual devotion.

Finally, she found her voice again. "We should probably find the elevator," she joked lightly, pointing down the hall.

"Right," Alex said, his arm slipping firmly around her waist. "Let's get out of here. We have our whole future to talk about tonight, and I'd rather do it somewhere cozier than a museum corridor."

His words made her heart flutter. *Our whole future.* In that moment, Maia knew: they might have faced their share of heartbreak before, but now, they were stepping together into something bright and limitless.

CHAPTER TWENTY-TWO

The aroma of roast duck and sweet-and-sour chicken hung deliciously in the air, drifting from the kitchen into the cozy dining room where Alex and Maia sat side by side. Light from the hanging lantern fixture shone warmly on the dishes laid out before them: shining platters of steaming meat, tender dumplings arranged in neat rows, and bowls brimming with stir-fried vegetables. Each dish bore the telltale sign of his parents' careful preparation—the vibrant colors and sumptuous smells that made their family restaurant so popular.

Across the table, Alex's father tucked into a generous helping of noodles, while his mother looked on with satisfaction at the gathering before her. For as long as Alex could remember, *family dinner night* meant bustling conversation and an abundance of food. Tonight, though, they had gone above and beyond, eager to meet Maia properly—his parents had insisted on serving her their best.

Maia gazed at the spread with childlike wonder, her eyes dancing over the countless dishes. "It smells as good as it looks. Oh my God." Her voice betrayed a giddy excitement that Alex found incredibly endearing.

He grinned, using chopsticks to place slices of roast duck onto his own plate. "Don't spend too much time admiring it, or it'll go cold on you." Then, with a flick of his wrist, he added two dumplings to her bowl. "Start eating before I devour it all myself."

Maia giggled, but she didn't hesitate to reach for her chopsticks. Meanwhile, his father scooped a mountain of sweet and sour chicken onto his plate, the glossy sauce coating each piece. Alex couldn't help but smile. A single glance at his father's plate proved how thoroughly he was enjoying dinner.

Maia fiddled with her phone, lifting it toward the table. "I have to get a photo before we dig in," she said, cheeks glowing with excitement. She snapped a quick shot of the glistening platters and turned the screen toward Alex. "Look at that—worthy of a cooking show, right?"

Alex leaned over to look, appreciating not just the image but the light in Maia's eyes. He teased in a hushed voice, "Go on and post it; I'll like it a thousand times if I can." If there was one thing he'd never tire of, it was being Maia's biggest supporter.

"I don't want anything left," Alex's mom said, patting her hands eagerly. She nodded toward the full plate she'd served herself—a generous helping of nearly every dish. "You two should eat as much as you want, and then some, because we made all this just for tonight."

While Alex's mother spoke, her gaze lingered fondly on Maia, as though trying to memorize every detail of her soon-to-be daughter-in-law's face. *Even if it was still early,* Alex could sense how wholly his parents had embraced Maia's presence. The fact that his mom had hugged Maia for an extra-long moment earlier had only confirmed it.

Maia chuckled, tapping her chopsticks together. "Don't underestimate me, Mrs. Zhang. My appetite can be pretty impressive. Alex can tell you all about the first time I ate at your restaurant."

He couldn't keep a laugh from escaping as he recounted that day. "She devoured her entire order—and then some," he said, recalling how her wide-eyed delight over the menu had charmed him from the start.

"I learned my lesson and taught myself to use chopsticks in preparation for tonight," Maia added, demonstrating her technique with a dumpling. She beamed when she noticed Alex's parents observing with approval. "I figured it'd be rude not to enjoy your amazing food in the traditional way."

Alex's mom clapped her hands gently, her eyes shining. "Look at that! Such grace. And I'm happy my son was patient enough to teach you."

Alex shrugged with a playful grin. "Mom, you know you raised me well. I'm not that big of a jerk."

His mother raised a pointed finger in mock scolding. "*We* didn't raise you to be a jerk at all, thank you very much." She turned back to Maia with interest. "So, my dear, how is it at the insurance agency? Busy?"

Maia paused mid-chew, lifting a finger politely to finish what she was eating before answering. "Yes, definitely. Some days are smoother than others, but the office can get… intense. Especially right after any big storm or accident—clients start filing claims like crazy."

"I see," Mrs. Zhang answered, leaning in. "And you also own two houses, right?" She glanced briefly at Alex, a gleam of excitement in her eyes.

Alex suppressed a groan. He had told them about Maia inheriting property, and ever since, his dad's inner business guru had been brimming with enthusiasm about the possibilities. "Yeah," Alex said, slipping seamlessly into the conversation. "She inherited one from her aunt, and we've actually been thinking about moving in… together."

He heard the soft gasp from both parents and felt Maia shift next to him. She straightened her back, her expression growing earnest. "Yes. We started fixing it up little by little. It's become a kind of weekend project." She glanced at Alex, warmth radiating through her gaze. "It means a lot to me, and to us, really. There's something about that place—it feels like a part of our story."

Alex nodded, images of them painting walls together, rummaging through old boxes, and dreaming aloud of how each room might look. "We're thinking it could become our home. A place to build new memories. You know, we're both runners—and this house is… sort of our *finish line*," he said, half-smiling at the metaphor. "Like another step in something we share."

Maia reached for her glass of lemonade and lifted it in a small toast. "And I know my aunt would've wanted me to make good use of it. If it brings us closer together, I think she'd be proud."

Mrs. Zhang's hand flew to her heart. "You two sound like something out of a romance novel," she declared, her face alight. "I don't think I've seen a pair this well-matched in real life."

With a decisive nod, she added, "Not like that manipulative girl… I've said it once, I'll say it a thousand times—*I never liked Phoebe.*"

Alex winced inwardly. *So much for not bringing her up.* His dad cleared his throat, muttering, "Here we go again," in a low voice.

But Maia smiled, somehow steering the conversation gracefully away from mention of his ex, joking lightly with his mom until the tension evaporated. Alex sat back, letting the lively chatter wash over him. Each time Maia laughed or teased his parents, his heart squeezed a little tighter. She fit with them so naturally. *Everything about her was a perfect complement to his life.*

His gaze swept over her as she happily engaged his mom in conversation, her hair brushing her shoulders whenever she nodded with interest. The overhead light illuminated her features in a soft glow, and Alex couldn't help remembering the moment he'd confessed his love not too long ago—and she'd returned it. *He closed his eyes briefly, feeling the warmth that memory always stirred.* He was a man in love, and it felt both terrifying and exhilarating.

THE CLANG of plates in the sink signaled that dinner was over. As the table cleared, Maia stood to collect dishes. His mother, of course, waved her off in polite refusal at first—until Maia insisted she truly didn't mind helping. With a grateful grin, Mrs. Zhang led her into the kitchen, the two women already talking animatedly about dish soaps and marinade recipes.

Alex exhaled, an odd mix of relief and nerves swirling in his chest. He and his father, arms loaded with empty plates and utensils, followed behind. After setting everything by the sink, Alex turned to his dad. "Hey, Dad, you mind if we talk in the living room for a second?"

His father quirked a brow but agreed without hesitation. Together, they stepped away from the busy kitchen, heading into the living room where a comfortable settee and matching armchair faced a modest TV. The overhead lamp cast a warm, homey light on the patterned carpet. Alex paused, straining his ears to ensure Maia and his mother were occupied. Sure enough, the cheerful sound of running water and clinking dishes floated in.

"What's on your mind, son?" his father asked, eyebrows raised. He placed a hand on Alex's shoulder with a gentle squeeze. "You're looking a little anxious. Are you worried we were too pushy?"

Alex found himself fiddling with an invisible thread on his sleeve. "I just... I needed advice, actually." He made sure his voice was low enough not to carry back to the kitchen. "Dad, when did you know you wanted to marry Mom?"

The question made his father's mouth twitch into a broad

smile. "Oh, that." He scratched his stubbly chin, eyes gleaming with nostalgia. "I knew after a week of dating her."

Alex blinked. "A week?"

His father laughed, clapping him on the back. "Sometimes it doesn't take long. I asked her right away. Crazy, maybe, but I had no regrets—clearly." He spread his hands, gesturing at the home they'd built and the family they'd become.

Alex swallowed, the comforting words dissolving some of his tension. "So… you really just *knew?*"

His dad's expression softened. "That's right. And by the look in your eyes, I'd say you know, too. Maia's good for you, son—and it's obvious you're good for her. You've been smiling like a man who found a missing piece he didn't realize he needed."

As if on cue, Alex felt the corners of his mouth turning up. He dared to let the image unfold in his mind: Maia in a white dress, stepping toward him with that radiant smile, the house they'd been fixing up turning into their first home as a married couple. The vision made his pulse pound. "I want to call her my wife," he murmured, almost testing how the words felt on his tongue.

His father grinned. "Then ask her. Don't overcomplicate it. If you love her, if she loves you—take the next step."

As simply as that, the advice was given. But the weight of it sank into Alex's heart. *She's been married before*, a small voice reminded him. She might not be so eager to jump in again. The memory of his own divorce still stung, though far less now that Maia had helped him mend. *What if she wasn't ready for marriage a second time?* A flicker of doubt cast a shadow over his excitement. But he knew he'd rather try than live with the question forever.

He inhaled deeply, nodding at his father. "You're right. I'll do it. I'll ask her." The words still triggered a trembling in his chest, but it was a thrilling kind of fear.

With another clap on the shoulder, his father wandered back toward the kitchen. Alex stayed behind, staring at the patterned carpet, letting the rush of thoughts settle. *Better to risk it all than stay silent.* Maia deserved to know how serious he was about their future.

From the other room, he heard her bright laughter. *Her laugh is my favorite sound*, he realized, sure beyond doubt that if he could secure that joy in his life forever, he would.

"Alex, look!" Maia called from the kitchen. She stood at the sink, soap-sudded fingers raised comically to resemble a strange, foamy sculpture. Even from across the room, he caught the delight dancing in her eyes. "Doesn't this look like one of those abstract pieces at the museum? It's practically art!"

His mother chuckled beside her, rinsing plates with a practiced hand. The moment Alex entered, he felt the warmth of domestic harmony—the cozy bustle, the gentle camaraderie of loved ones working together. It tugged at his heart.

Alex grinned and jogged toward them, coming up behind Maia to fold an arm around her waist. He leaned forward to plant a quick kiss on her cheek, inhaling the faint floral note of her shampoo beneath the smell of lemon-scented dish soap. "Sculpture or not, you're going to get bubbles all over the floor," he teased gently.

She laughed and handed him a towel. "Then come help before I start an art exhibit we can't clean up."

His father had already begun drying plates and stacking them neatly. Alex took up another towel, slipping into the routine like he'd done countless times before—but *this time* it felt different. Maia was there, right in the thick of it, seamlessly fitting in with his family. She giggled at his mom's stories, bantered with his dad, and beamed whenever Alex caught her eye.

He couldn't stop a soft ache of love from spreading through

him. *Soon,* he vowed silently, as he brushed a stray soapy bubble off Maia's forearm. *I'm going to make you my wife—and I won't be afraid to ask.*

CHAPTER TWENTY-THREE

Maia smoothed the silky fabric of her dress, letting her fingers trail over the delicate lace overlay. The color was a muted rose-gold that shimmered under the slightest light, and every time she moved, the dress seemed to ripple like liquid. *Thank you, Aimee,* she thought, recalling the hours they'd spent in various boutiques, searching for something that would strike the perfect note of elegance. Tonight marked her and Alex's first official night living together, and she wanted to look exceptional.

She approached Aunt Dianne's home—no, *their* home now—with a bubbling mixture of excitement and nerves. Though she and Alex had been dating for six months, this was a new level of intimacy: sharing a home, waking up in the same space, walking through these halls day after day as they built their future. Her heart fluttered at the thought.

When she reached the porch, she stopped short. The warm glow of two scented candles flickered invitingly at either end of the welcome mat. *Rose petals?* She blinked in delight, realizing they were scattered across the mat in a neat arrangement, releasing a faint, sweet aroma that mingled with the fresh evening air. "Oh my gosh," she breathed, pressing a palm lightly to her chest. *Could her boyfriend be any more remarkable?*

She stepped carefully over the petals, balanced on her tall heels, and unlocked the front door. "Honey, I'm home!" she called, amusement flooding her voice. The words felt a little silly, but they also held a thrill: for the first time in years, she felt a surge of genuine excitement at saying them.

Inside, everything was hushed except for the faint crackle of candles. The space she'd spent so long helping to renovate was transformed, dimmed lights casting the newly polished floors in a warm, golden glow. Another trail of rose petals led from the entryway to the living room and into the kitchen, and Maia followed it eagerly. Each step sent a pleasant awareness through her body—*this is real; we are truly living together now.*

At the threshold of the kitchen, she gasped. Candles perched on the countertops, bathing the room in a gentle, flickering light. A small table was set in the center, its surface adorned with a crisp white tablecloth and carefully laid place settings. Two gold-rimmed plates shone under the candlelight, and a single bottle of wine stood as the centerpiece. It was a scene straight out of a fairytale.

Suddenly, movement to her left caught her eye. Alex emerged from the shadows, a single rose clasped between two fingers like some dashing hero in an old romance film. He wore a tuxedo of deep navy, perfectly tailored to his broad shoulders and long frame. The crisp white shirt beneath and the slight gleam of polished shoes completed the look. Maia's breath caught at the sight of him.

"My beautiful Maia has made it home," he greeted softly, his voice carrying a playful warmth. The rose in his hand swayed gently as he stepped toward her.

Emotion welled up in Maia's chest—gratitude, excitement, love. She bit her lower lip, a grin lighting her face. Words failed her for a moment, so she simply crossed the room and wrapped her arms around him. His familiar warmth and the light hint of his cologne instantly put her at ease.

He squeezed her in return, pressing a quick kiss to her lips. "Do you like the flowers?" he asked, voice filled with a note of boyish hope.

"*Like* them?" She placed a hand to her heart, glancing around the softly illuminated kitchen once more. "They're perfect. And you've outdone yourself, Alex."

He gestured for her to stay put as he moved to pull out a chair at the candlelit table. "Oh, I'm just getting started," he teased, that mischievous twinkle in his eyes making her pulse quicken.

But before she could settle in the offered seat, something on the chair caught her eye—*her old running shoes*. Frayed at the edges from countless jogs, they rested against the cushion. Her brow furrowed in confusion. "Wait, where did you find these?" She stepped over to Alex's chair and spotted *his* old pair, too—equally worn, the treads practically smooth from all their miles together. "Um, are we planning to run around the house instead of eating?" she joked, trying to piece together his intention.

Alex only tapped at his phone, which sat upright on the counter next to a new toaster they'd bought earlier that week. In response, a gentle R&B melody began to play from a hidden speaker. The smooth chords and pulsing bassline seemed to wrap around them, transforming the kitchen into a private dance hall.

The singer's voice flowed through the air, caressing Maia's ears: *When you chose me, my life began.* She felt her heart flutter at the lyrics. Alex took a step closer, wearing a soft smile that made her knees feel unsteady.

"This song is amazing," Maia murmured, setting her purse on the counter before swaying gently to the rhythm. She couldn't resist the urge to move as the beat sank into her bones.

Her fingers curled around the hem of her dress to keep it from swishing too high.

A moment later, she felt Alex's hand on her waist—light, tentative—and she let herself melt into him. They began to dance, footsteps slow and careful in the flicker of candlelight. He twirled her gracefully, letting her skirt fan out, then pulled her close so that she could rest her head against his chest. The steady thump of his heartbeat echoed in her ear, a comforting sound that made her feel utterly safe.

They'd shared so many experiences in the six months of their relationship—jogs at dawn, impromptu dinner dates, family dinners with his folks—but they'd never really danced. *This moment feels like everything,* she thought, allowing the warmth of his embrace and the sweet croon of the singer's voice to lull her into pure contentment.

As the chorus swelled, Alex eased her away slightly, just enough so she could meet his gaze. He pressed his forehead gently against hers, the subtle brush of his hair sending a soft tingle across her skin. "Did the shoes remind you of anything?" he asked, the question delicate as a caress.

A small laugh escaped her, and she reached out to run her fingertips across the battered sneakers on the chair. "They take me back to when we first started running together. It was so new, and we'd both just come out of heartbreak. Those shoes—*these shoes*—carried us through the early mornings, the first real conversations, the doubts, and the wins." Her eyes moved back to him, brimming with affection. "They remind me of *us*—how far we've come, and how many more miles we want to run side by side."

A thoughtful glimmer lit Alex's eyes. "Exactly," he said, voice low and earnest. "I've never thought of jogging as a literal metaphor for moving forward in life until I met you. We've both faced hurt, but we decided to push ahead—together." He lowered his voice further, the sincerity in his words bringing a tingle to her spine. "I want to keep moving forward with you, always."

Her heart pounded a wild rhythm as he slipped one hand into his suit pocket. Her breath caught. *Is this...*

When he drew out a small black box and held it between them, Maia's entire body went still, as though the world had momentarily stopped spinning. Candlelight glinted off the box's smooth surface, and she could just make out a ring inside, shining with quiet brilliance.

"Maia," Alex said gently. His gaze never wavered from hers, and the steadiness in his expression made her feel like she could face anything in the world. "Will you do me the greatest honor anyone ever could? Will you agree to be my jogging partner in life—forever—by marrying me?"

For an instant, a dizzying wave of emotion swelled in her chest, stealing her breath and making her vision blur with unshed tears. She pressed both hands over her mouth, warmth blooming across her body like sunlight. The ring—simple yet undeniably beautiful—sparkled in the flickering glow. *He wants to marry me.* Her mind raced over every memory, every day they'd spent together, how he'd listened so deeply to her hurts and joys, how he'd never let her doubts push him away. *This is the man I trust with my whole heart.*

She didn't need to think twice. Removing her hands from her mouth, she let out a small, breathless laugh. "Yes," she managed, voice trembling with happiness. "Alex, I'd be... so happy to be your wife." Tears pricked her eyes, but she welcomed them, letting them express the gratitude and certainty flooding her. *No fear—just hope.* "I want that more than anything. Thank you for believing in me, in us."

His own relief shone in his eyes. Tenderly, he slid the ring onto her finger, the cool metal settling into place as though it had always belonged there. Maia couldn't help but gaze at it, enthralled by how it symbolized every promise they were making.

He cupped her face in his palm, leaning in to kiss her with a gentle reverence that sent sparks through her veins. They stood there in the softly lit kitchen, the romantic melody still enveloping them, candles flickering around them like silent witnesses to this life-altering moment.

Maia clung to Alex's lapels, heart pounding, aware that she was stepping into a chapter of her life she'd once feared would never happen again—a chapter filled with love, commitment, and endless possibility. And, as she held his gaze, warmth and tears threatening to overflow, she knew she was exactly where she needed to be.

EPILOGUE

An orange leaf clung to the glass wall beside the booth, stark against the diner's interior. The gusty wind outside pressed the leaf there for a moment, as if trying to peek into the cozy space within. Maia watched it flutter before her gaze drifted to the people milling behind the window. Despite the brisk weather, Sweetgum was abuzz with anticipation for the fall festival later in the day. Bright posters decorated every storefront, announcing live music, local crafts, and—if the rumors were true—some big surprises.

She breathed in the comforting scent of her steaming coffee, letting the warmth spread through her palms. Her mind wandered to the festival's events and how the entire town seemed electrified by the season: the swirl of leaves in reds, oranges, and yellows, the comforting smell of cinnamon drifting from the bakery across the street, and the knowledge that by evening, Main Street would be transformed into a vibrant tapestry of autumn delights.

Click, click, click.

The sound of boots on the tiled floor made Maia glance up. Aimee approached, wearing an oversized knit sweater and a harried expression. "There she is," Maia cooed, though it was clear her friend was anything but relaxed. "Who's ready to head out? Alex is waiting for us at town square."

She half-expected Aimee to spring to action, but instead her friend collapsed into the seat across from her, stretching her arms across the table with an exasperated sigh. The sleeves of her sweater scrunched up at the elbows.

"Oh my God. Today has been insane," Aimee groaned, her eye giving a little twitch that betrayed her stress.

Maia arched an eyebrow, surprised to see her so frazzled. Although the diner was relatively calm at the moment, she remembered how hectic things had become in recent months. Rochelle's upcoming retirement had turned the place into a magnet for locals wanting to grab one last meal from the woman who'd fed the town's residents for decades. Throw in the gossip about Rochelle's mysterious "nephew" taking over, and everyone seemed eager to catch a glimpse of this unseen heir-apparent—whenever he finally arrived.

"What do you mean?" Maia asked, taking a thoughtful sip of coffee. She tipped her head toward the far side of the diner, where Old Man Benjamin was hunched over his usual table, nursing a bowl of soup. "Did your new favorite regular come in again, or did Mr. Benjamin manage to pop a blood vessel for you?"

Aimee cast a pointed look down the aisle, but her lips quirked in a grudging smile. "Mr. Benjamin has been fine— cantankerous as always, but not the culprit." She rose, straightening her sweater sleeves. "And, for the record, that so-called *favorite regular* is more of a pain than anything." Rolling her eyes, she lifted her phone to check the time. "We really should get going. I was supposed to be off fifteen minutes ago, but everything ran late."

Taking the hint, Maia quickly downed the rest of her coffee. The taste of roasted beans lingered on her tongue as she stood, automatically glancing at the engagement ring on her finger. Even after nine months, the sight of it still gave her a pleasant flutter in her stomach. It felt so natural—and yet so exciting. In another year (maybe sooner, if they could get the planning done), she'd walk down the aisle to Alex. *This is really happening.*

Her mind flickered to all those evenings spent in their new shared home, huddled together, discussing color schemes, guest lists, and invitations. "All right, let's go," she said with a bright smile, following Aimee out of the diner and onto the breezy sidewalk.

Outside, Sweetgum was well into its autumn makeover: store windows were lined with pumpkins, gourds, and swirling leaf garlands. The streetlamps had bundles of corn stalks tied around them, and folks bustled past, clad in warm sweaters and jackets in shades of burgundy, rust, and olive. A pleasant crispness filled the air, carrying a faint hint of apple cider and woodsmoke.

Side by side, Maia and Aimee walked toward the town square, chatting about the festival events—a pie-eating contest, a hayride, live music on a makeshift stage. Several volunteers scurried about, sweeping away the stubborn leaves that seemed determined to cling to the sidewalks. Maia found the seasonal chaos comforting, a reminder of how Sweetgum rallied together for these hometown celebrations.

Sure enough, when they reached the square, Alex was there, leaning against a wooden barricade. He scrolled through his phone, probably checking event updates or responding to messages. A small surge of happiness welled in Maia's chest at the sight of him, dressed in a thick sweater that highlighted his broad shoulders. *He's waiting for us,* she thought. *He's always there, waiting—just like he said he would be.*

"Afternoon, honey," he greeted when he saw her, and she rose onto her toes to kiss him lightly. A pleasant warmth spread through her at the familiar gesture, the comfort of belonging.

She slid an arm around him, nestling her cheek against the soft knit of his sweater, savoring his cozy warmth in the chill air.

Aimee gave them a friendly wave. "Hey, Alex. How's your day been?"

He slipped his phone into his pocket, returning her wave. "Pretty good, actually. Been looking forward to meeting you both here. I wanted to see the festival start getting set up." He gestured at the stage, where a handful of people busily adjusted microphones and arranged speakers.

Maia snuggled closer, hugging Alex's waist. "Kinda feels like we've made you a third wheel, though," she teased, peering at Aimee with a playful smile.

Aimee rolled her eyes but in good humor. "Please, I'm perfectly fine snapping pictures and letting you two be nauseatingly adorable," she retorted, though there was a slight wistfulness in her eyes. She lifted her phone, taking pictures of the small crowd and the stage. "I'll just be your personal photographer, capturing all the cuteness."

Alex, ever observant, gave her arm a supportive pat. "Sometimes love appears at the most unexpected times. Trust me. It happened to me," he said, exchanging a fond look with Maia that made her heart flutter. "You never know what new face might walk into your life, especially around Sweetgum."

"Sure," Aimee sighed, clearly unconvinced but trying to rally her spirits. She pointed toward a group of volunteers setting up orange-and-black booths along the street. "Look, they're already putting everything together. The festival's going to be great—I remember last year's was a blast."

As Aimee got lost in describing the caramel apple stand and the costume contest from the previous fall, Maia's gaze flicked between her friend and Alex. She had a sneaking suspicion that maybe, just maybe, Aimee's love story was on the horizon. *Who knows?* Romance had a habit of sneaking up when people least expected it, and Maia found herself quietly wishing her friend would soon experience the same wonder she'd found with Alex.

The idea made her laugh softly—envisioning Aimee's "knight in shining armor" showing up out of nowhere, perhaps as Rochelle's rumored nephew or even as that *favorite regular* Aimee kept complaining about. The thought was too delicious not to consider. *She might be fuming now, but maybe they'll hit it off...*

She let out a small chuckle, feeling Alex's hand tighten around hers. "Everything okay?" he asked, his voice gentle, leaning down so only she could hear.

She nodded, looking up at him. His warm brown eyes glowed with affection—an unspoken reminder of the journey they'd taken to get here. From two broken hearts bonding over morning jogs to forging a life together, they'd come so far. "I'm just thinking how glad I am that I found you," she murmured, squeezing his hand.

He touched his forehead to hers in a moment of tenderness that felt entirely private, despite the bustling festival around them. "Same page, Maia," he replied, echoing a phrase that always made her heart skip. "Always the same page."

His words filled her with hope. She turned back to watch Aimee snapping photos of the stage as the band began a sound-check, the music faint but promising. The cool wind carried the aroma of roasting chestnuts and warm cider from nearby stalls. In the distance, a banner flapped in the breeze, announcing *Sweetgum Fall Festival* in cheery letters. The crowd around them grew thicker, brimming with laughter and conversation as the day's events ramped up.

Maia inhaled the crisp autumn air, eyes drifting over the excited faces streaming into the square. *This is home,* she thought, heart brimming with contentment. She had a partner she adored, a town that felt like an extended family, and a future bright with possibilities. *And who knows what tomorrow might bring?*

She caught a glimpse of Aimee glancing back, that wistful spark dancing behind her smile. Maia's chest fluttered with anticipation for her friend's next chapter—whatever it would be, Maia knew in her heart that in Sweetgum, anything could happen.

AUTHOR'S NOTE

Thank you so much for reading Endless Love, the eighth book in the Sweetgum Meadows Romance series of stand-alone novels. I really hope you loved it! If you enjoyed this book, please consider leaving it a review so that others may also find it. Also, if you haven't read the first seven books, yet, check them out today! Although these are stand-alone novels, the stories all intertwine and progress.

I look forward to introducing you to the other characters in this lovely, family-oriented town where each couple will find their happily ever after.

Would you like to receive bonus scenes and keep up with what's next with my upcoming books? Then, make sure you sign up for my mailing list on my website by visiting ImaniPrice.com.

To all my lovely readers,

Thank you for reading

www.ingramcontent.com/pod-product-compliance
Lightning Source LLC
Chambersburg PA
CBHW061349310726
48974CB00001B/271